BULL
{ WE MAKE IT HAPPEN }

JARRETT HALEY }} EDITOR

MANAGING EDITOR {{ JARED YATES SEXTON

KAJ TANAKA / JOSH PETERSON }} ASST. EDITORS

WEB EDITOR {{ CHRISTOPHER WOLFORD

PETE WITTE }} BULL{SHOT} EDITOR

NON-FICTION EDITOR {{ LUCAS AHLSEN

CURTIS DAWKINS }} BOOK REVIEWS

SOCIAL {{ DAVE FITZPATRICK / CONNOR FURGUSON

JAMES-ALEXANDER MATHERS }} COVER ART

ILLUSTRATOR {{ ANTHONY SCHECHTMAN

BRADY JACKSON }} DESIGN

EDITORIAL BOARD {{ RYAN BRADLEY
RACHEL DARK / BENJAMIN DREVLOW
MICHAEL GOODELL / ELISE GRUNEISEN
MCKENZIE HIGHTOWER / CHARLES LABUZ
NICHOLAS SCOTT / CHRIS WIEWIORA

№ 4

BULL © 2014
All rights reserved.
ISBN: 978-1-938012-05-1 | ISSN: 2165-0853
For subscriptions and inquiries visit:
www.BULLmensfiction.com

{TABLE OF CONTENTS}

- ★ **CATFIGHT** {6}
  DEVIN MURPHY

- ★ **APOCRYPHA** {13}
  RICHARD LANGE

- ★ **LIPSTICK AND HANDCUFFS** {35}
  MICHAEL HEMMINGSON

- ★ **HEAD** {41}
  DARRIN DOYLE

- ★ **TARZAN IN SPACE** {59}
  ANTHONY MALONE

- ★ **THE BULL INTERVIEW: CURTIS DAWKINS** {79}
  JARRETT HALEY

- ★ **RIMER'S BOOTS** {91}
  COLIN FLEMING

- ★ **THE NAZI METHOD** {113}
  CHARLEY HENLEY

- ★ **THE ONYX SKULL** {133}
  TIM DICKS

- ★ **CONTRIBUTORS** {158}

Illustrations by Anthony Schechtman / anthonyshechtman.tumblr.com
Cover art by James-Alexander Mathers / jamathers.com
Issue design by Brady Jackson / bradyisbrady.com

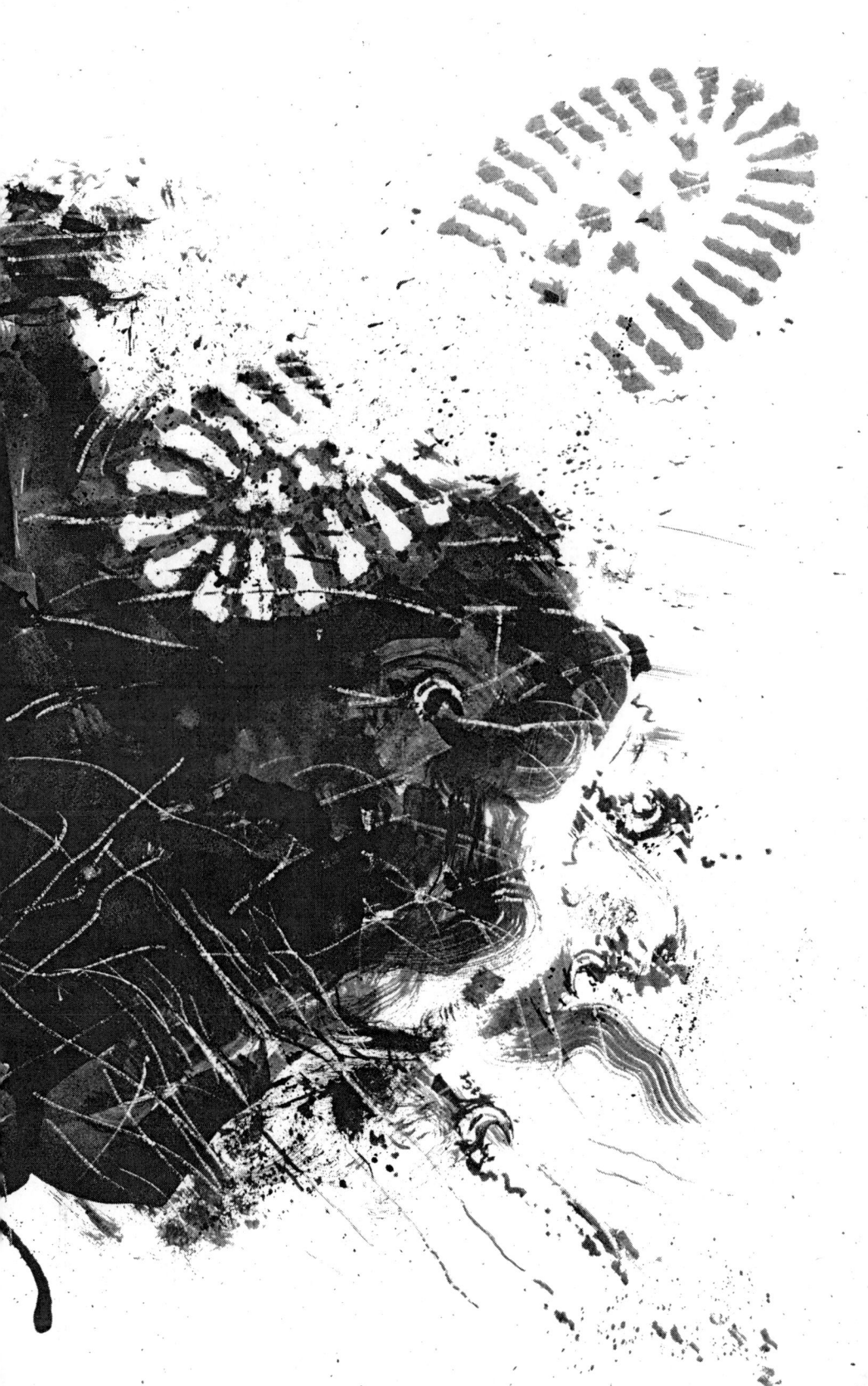

CATFIGHT

DEVIN MURPHY

IT WAS A BET brought Lance and me to the SPCA. I didn't know what SPCA stood for and I'm not really sure even now. But our bar had closed and we all trucked over and Glen Brim had the keys. He was the rare kind of roughneck who bothered to work during his months off the rig—nights as a janitor hosing cat piss off cages. Kevin Clayton and Don Kowalski and about two dozen others were there, all half-blasted on boilermakers. Jarhead Johnny kept saying, "Will ya look at that one," as Glen dumped one feral cat after another into the glass-walled visiting room. And you wouldn't believe all them cats. Different breeds and colors lined the walls and a big 'ol Maine Coon hunched right in the middle because there wasn't more space to hide with all the others hissing and swatting at each other.

When the cats were all in Glen waved Lance forward and the men parted to make a path to the door. Lance had on his steel-toed work boots, a pair of faded black Carhartt pants, no shirt, and these blue snorkeling goggles God knows where he got 'em. There was a small chalkboard with over/under odds written across the top. If he got through all thirty-four cats in ten minutes he won seven thousand dollars. That was the deal.

This was on overlap night, when the crew finishing and starting a contract get put up in the same hotel before being flown home or ferried to the rigs. Those leaving are flush with cash, ten or twenty drinks deep, and dying of boredom from the monotony of working months straight.

Lance glanced at me before stepping into the cat room. We'd met working rotations on offshore rigs in the Gulf and had bunked together for the last three years, so I'd known him long enough to see he didn't want to do what he was about to do anymore. Though he didn't say a word.

I stood up against the glass.

Then Glen yelled, "Go!" and the other men began hammering on the windows trying to get them cats agitated.

For a second Lance didn't know what to do. I mean, these cats are all up on those carpeted towers or wedging themselves into the corners. So he walks over and when he wraps his fingers around the top of some poor Calico's neck, another cat bolts up his shin, grapples onto the flesh of his inner thigh. He swats at it and the cat scrambles up his back, wedging under his right arm and I saw its needle teeth sink into his shoulder blade. Lance yells and I swear the cat looked like it was really enjoying all this, hunting or something, or just getting into the sport of it, till Lance yanked it loose by the tail. It found his forearm and scratched red grooves down it before he swung the thing over his head and onto the floor, skull hitting the concrete with a sick thud.

Lance chucked the mess at all of us against the window. The men standing there cheered to see the streaked column of blood.

He was breathing heavy and grunted as he slipped on the dead cat's blood, got up and slipped again.

Lance specializes in welding valves and piping so he pretty much squeezes steel with his hands all day long. His arms are just cords of veins. All that strength starts rising out of him in the room and he gets to moving faster, gliding from one corner to the other of the visiting room stomping on 'em, punting the ones he can't catch, and scooping up the ones he could and twisting their necks, which probably sounded awful but couldn't be heard over the men pounding glass and screaming. For every cat Lance got his hands on, two or three got ahold of him, giving him these arch-backed, frenzied claw strikes.

Four minutes in and his shoulders and chest are almost as bloody as the floor. But once he got the hang of it his body took over, all quick-twitch muscle and instinct. He palmed an orange tabby by the head and split it open against the tile wall like a young coconut. He pulled at the white boots of a black cat's fore and hind legs until they were taught and snapped its spine against his rising knee before moving on, leaving mangled critters all over the floor.

And I'm not kidding, he finished in time to win the money.

When it was over we brought him to the little operating table that could barely hold half of him. He laid there with his legs hanging off the side while Jimmy MacKale, a paramedic, tweezed out the little claws and the pinkish teeth all broken off in Lance's skin.

"Good Lord, look at that," Jarhead Johnny said, as they shot tetanus into Lance's abdomen and poured iodine over his chest, spots of it bubbling up like root beer foam that browned the skin.

The rest of the men left wads of cash in a filthy pile under a poster of a happy family holding brindled mutt. They left the building and got in their trucks like this was any old Saturday night, which I guess it was.

Lance's gauze pads went pink from soaking up the puddles of

watered down blood on the surface of the vet's table. And because I said I'd help long before I really knew what that meant, Glen tossed me a pair of yellow dish gloves and I picked up the Maine Coon by the scruff of its neck. The tail fur had dark and smoky gray rings. Its fractured-marble eyes caught the dead fluorescent light overhead as I lowered it into one of the two fifty-gallon trash bins.

When all the cats were in the bins, Glen ran a hose in and sprayed the room off. Blood, fur and broken claws pooled over the drain, and shame clawed over my shoulder as I cleared the clotted grating with my boot.

When we finished cleaning the gray floors looked darker when wet. A lone dog was barking somewhere in the back. We used Glen's van to drive outside of town to the Red River on the Texas border.

"I fish here," Glen said as his van rocked over a dirt path through the darkened trees. Lance leaned against the passenger side door and groaned every time we hit an exposed root.

"You sure you're not going to die on me?" Glen asked. He jawed away our whole drive. Words came easy to him. But I couldn't imagine ever telling anyone about what we'd just seen. I had no one to listen to the stories I'd collected anyway. In Alaska, I'd felt weather so cold that the sap froze deep in the trees and made the trunks explode. Out in the Gulf of Mexico a flaming oil slick got sucked up by a small cyclone and the tower of flame traveled over the ocean like God's finger. I'd seen a scared man destroy thirty-four cats at a time but what did any of it really do for my life?

GLEN BACKED UP HIS van to the bank of the Red River and the two of us pulled out the cans. Glen uncapped the first bin, pulled one out by the tail, rocked it behind him and tossed it far enough out that it would flow downstream. The river was glowing silver—black in the shadow, translucent when you looked straight at it, with perfectly round stones all along the bottom. Under such big skies and on such vast stretches of land I came to see the place around me as a sort of holy thing and it seemed a sin to act anything other than reverent. But we threw the cats into the water just the same, walking to the edge with two at a time and sailing them into the air. Most sunk under. An exotic longhair was swept twenty yards downstream and molded to a rounded rock like a wet bathmat.

After we were done, I walked upstream, stripped down to my boxers and waded into the river over algae-slicked stones until the water rolled off my shoulders and my limbs went numb from the cold. On one bank was Louisiana, and on the other Texas. Glen helped Lance with his shirt and pants and they walked into the river. Lance's upper body was bandaged like an unraveling mummy from the neck down, and both of Glen's arms were sleeved in tattoos.

Watching them it was clear that they were my kind, that my life was to be spent around hard bitten men with oddball hieroglyphs and scars carved into our bodies and speaking of so many lives. All our days spent on rigs, or otherwise within the stink of refineries with the petroleum glow shimmering above the purple cooling flames. Another life would be coming soon; there was money to be made working for natural gas companies in the Dakotas over the next few years. There was a big gas bubble running under both those states that was starting to look profitable since gas topped $4.00 a gallon. Those were the only numbers we knew. Our lives were governed by prices and those were the only reasons to change for men like us. I saw that as Glen lent himself to the water and Lance eased his shredded skin beneath the surface.

We were too old to be friends like this. We'd each blown it with women and nothing good was likely to come of the unions we made with each other. No combinations of sharing anythign but our burdens could amount to a family, and we should probably be left to ourselves.

The longhair was no longer stuck to the rock and the water held no sign of the cats. Someone downriver would think some strange ark had run aground, puncturing the hull and flooding the holds, sending this animal cargo flowing downstream. I dunked my head under again and wanted the river to rise higher and take me away, to rise higher and take us all. But it didn't, and when I looked around at the tree-lined banks rustling in the dawn I thought how goddamned beautiful this world would be if we had never been allowed to touch it, and the three of us kept wading in the cold river like children without anyone to call us home.

APOCRYPHA

RICHARD LANGE

If I had money, I'd go to Mexico. Not Tijuana or Ensenada, but farther down, real Mexico. Get my ass out of L.A. There was this guy in the Army, Marcos, who was from a little town on the coast called Mazunte. He said you could live pretty good there for practically nothing. Tacos were 50 cents, beers a buck.

"How do they feel about black folks?" I asked him.

"They don't care about anything but the color of your money," he said.

I already know how to speak enough Spanish to get by, how to ask for things and order food. Por favor and muchas gracias. The numbers to a hundred.

The Chinese family across the hall is always cooking in their room. I told Papa-san to cut it out, but he just stood there nodding and smiling with his little boy and little girl wrapped around his legs. The next day I saw Mama-san coming up the stairs with another bag of groceries, and this morning the whole floor smells like deep-fried fish heads again. I'm not an unreasonable man. I ignore that there are four of them living in a room meant for two, and I put up with the kids playing in the hall when I'm trying to sleep, but I'm not going to let them torch the building.

I pull on some pants and head downstairs. The elevator is broken, so it's four flights on foot. The elevator's always broken, or the toilet, or the sink. Roaches like you wouldn't believe too. The hotel was built in 1928, and nobody's done anything to it since. Why should they? There's just a bunch of poor niggers living here, Chinamen and wetbacks, dope fiends and drunks. Hell, I'm sure the men with the money are on their knees every night praying this heap falls down so they can collect on the insurance and put up something new.

The first person I see when I hit the lobby—the first person who sees me—is Alan. I call him Youngblood. He's the boy who sweeps the floors and hoses off the sidewalk.

"Hey, D, morning, D," he says, bouncing off the couch and coming at me. "Gimme a dollar, man. I'm hungry as a motherfucker."

I raise my hand to shut him up, walk right past him. I don't have time for his hustle today.

"They're cooking up there again," I say to the man at the desk, yell at him through the bulletproof glass. He's Chinese, too, and every month so are more of the tenants. I know what's going on, don't think I don't.

"Okay, I talk to them," the man says, barely looking up from his phone.

"It's a safety hazard," I say.

"Yeah, yeah, okay," he says.

"Yeah, yeah, okay to you," I say. "Next time I'm calling the fire department."

Youngblood is waiting for me when I finish. He's so skinny he uses one hand to hold up his jeans when he walks. Got fuzz in his hair, boogers in the corners of his eyes, and smells like he hasn't bathed in a week. That's what dope'll do to you.

"Come on, D, slide me a dollar, and I'll give you this," he says.

He holds out his hand. There's a little silver disc in his palm, smaller than a dime.

"What is it?" I say.

"It's a battery, for a watch," he says.

"And what am I supposed to do with it?"

"Come on, D, be cool."

Right then the front door opens, and three dudes come gliding in, the light so bright behind them they look like they're stepping out of the sun. I know two of them: J Bone, who stays down the hall from me, and his homeboy Dallas. A couple of grown-up crack babies, crazy as hell. The third one, the tall, good-looking kid in the suit and shiny shoes, is a stranger. He has an air about him like he doesn't belong down here, like he ought to be pulling that suitcase through an airport in Vegas or Miami. He moves and laughs like a high roller, a player, the kind of brother you feel good just standing next to.

He and his boys walk across the lobby, goofing on each other. When they get to the stairs, the player stops and says, "You mean I got to carry my shit up four floors?"

"I'll get it for you," J Bone says. "No problem."

The Chinaman at the desk buzzes them through the gate, and up they go, their boisterousness lingering for a minute like a pretty girl's perfume.

"Who was that?" I say mostly to myself.

"That's J Bone's cousin," Youngblood says. "Fresh outta County."

Trouble. Come looking for me again.

THE OLD MAN ASKS if I know anything about computers. He's sitting in his office in back, jabbing at the keys of the laptop his son bought him to use for inventory but that the old man mainly plays solitaire on. He picks the thing up and sets it down hard on his desk as if trying to smack some sense into it.

"Everything's stuck," he says.

"Can't help you there, Boss," I say. "I was out of school before they started teaching that stuff."

I'm up front in the showroom. I've been the security guard here for six years now, 10-6, Tuesday through Saturday. It's just me and the old man, day after day, killing time in the smallest jewelry store in the district, where he's lucky to buzz in ten customers a week. If I was 82 years old and had his money, I wouldn't be running out my string here, but his wife's dead, and his friends have moved away, and the world keeps changing so fast that I guess this is all he has left to anchor him, his trade, the last thing he knows by heart.

I get up out of my chair—he doesn't care if I sit when nobody's in the store—and tuck in my uniform. Every so often I like to stretch my legs with a stroll around the showroom. The old man keeps the display cases looking nice, dusts the rings and bracelets and watches every day, wipes down the glass. I test him now and then by leaving a thumbprint somewhere, and it's always gone the next morning.

Another game I play to pass the time, I'll watch the people walking past outside and bet myself whether the next one'll be black or Mexican, a man or a woman, wearing a hat or not, things like that. Or I'll lean my chair back as far as it'll go, see how long I can balance on the rear legs. The old man doesn't like that one, always yells, "Stop fidgeting. You make me nervous." And I've also learned to kind of sleep with my eyes open and my head up, half in this world, half in the other.

I walk over to the door and look outside. It's a hot day, and folks are keeping to the shade where they can. Some are waiting for a bus across the street, in front of the music store that blasts that *oom pah pah oom pah pah* all day long. Next to that's a McDonald's, then a bridal shop, then a big jewelry store with signs in the windows saying COMPRAMOS ORO, We Buy Gold.

A kid ducks into our doorway to get out of the sun. He's yelling into his phone in Spanish and doesn't see me standing on the other side of the glass, close enough I can count the pimples on his chin.

"*Por que?*" he says. That's "Why?" or sometimes "Because." "*Por que? Por que?*"

When he feels my eyes on him, he flinches, startled. I chuckle as he moves out to the curb. He glances over his shoulder a couple times like I'm something he's still not sure of.

"Is it too cold in here?" the old man shouts.

He's short already, but hunched over like he is these days, he's practically a midget. Got about ten white hairs left on his head, ears as big as a goddamn monkey's, and those kind of thick glasses that make your eyes look like they belong to someone else.

"You want me to dial it down?" I say.

"What about you? Are you cold?" he says.

"Don't worry about me," I say.

Irving Mandelbaum. I call him Mr. M or Boss. He's taken to using a cane lately, if he's going any distance, and I had to call 911 a while back when I found him face-down on the office floor. It was just a fainting spell, but I still worry.

"Five degrees then," he says. "If you don't mind."

I adjust the thermostat and return to my chair. When I'm sure Mr. M is in the office, I rock back and get myself balanced. My world record is three minutes and twenty-seven seconds.

I'VE BEEN LIVING IN the hotel a while now. Before that it was someplace worse, over on Fifth. Someplace where you had crackheads and hypes puking in the hallways and ODing in the bathrooms we shared. Someplace where you had women knocking on your door at all hours, asking could they suck your dick for five dollars. It was barely better than being on the street, which is where I ended up after my release from Lancaster. Hell, it was barely better than Lancaster.

A Mexican died in the room next to mine while I was living there. I was the one who found him, and how I figured it out was the smell. I was doing janitorial work in those days, getting home at dawn and sleeping all morning, or trying to anyway. At first the odor was just a tickle in my nostrils, but then I started to taste something in the air that made me gag if I breathed too deeply. I didn't think anything of it because it was the middle of summer and there was no air conditioning and half the time the showers were broken. To put it plainly, everybody stunk in that place. I went out and bought a couple of rose-scented deodorizers and set them next to my bed.

A couple of days later I was walking to my room when something strange on the floor in front of 316 caught my eye. I bent down for a closer look and one second later almost fell over trying to get up again. What it was was three fat maggots, all swole up like overcooked rice. I got down on my hands and knees and pressed my cheek to the floor to see under the door, and more maggots wriggled on the carpet inside the room, dancing around the dead man they'd sprung from.

Nobody would tell me how the guy died, but they said it was so hot in the room during the time he lay in there that he exploded. It took a special crew in white coveralls and rebreathers two days to clean up the mess, and even then the smell never quite went away. It was one of the happiest days of my life when I moved from there.

J-Bone's cousin, the player from the lobby, is laughing at me. His name is Leon. I'm not trying to be funny, but the man is high, so everything makes him laugh.

It's 6:30 in the afternoon outside. In here, with the tinfoil covering the windows, it might as well be midnight. I suspect time isn't the main thing on the minds of Leon and Bone and the two girls passing a blunt on the bed. They've been at it for hours already and seem to be planning on keeping the party going way past what's wise.

The door to Bone's room was wide open when I walked by after work, still wearing my uniform. I heard music playing, saw people sitting around.

"Who's that, McGruff the Crime Dog?" Leon called out.

Some places it's okay to keep going when you hear something like that. Not here. Here, if you give a man an inch on you, he'll most definitely take a mile. So I went back.

"What was that?" I said, serious but smiling, not weighting it one way or the other.

"Naw, man, naw," Leon said. "I was just fucking with you. Come on in and have a beer."

All I wanted was to get home and watch Jeopardy, but I couldn't say no now, now that Leon had backed down. I had to have at least one drink. One of the girls handed me a Natural Light, and Leon joked that I better not let anybody see me with it while I was in uniform.

"That's cops, man, not guards," I said, and that's what got him laughing.

"You know what though," he says. "Most cops be getting high as motherfuckers."

Everybody nods and murmurs, "That's right, that's right."

"I mean, who got the best dope?" he continues. "Cops' girlfriends, right?"

He's wearing the same suit he had on the other day, the shirt unbuttoned and the jacket hanging on the back of his chair. He's got the gift of always looking more relaxed than any man has a right to, and that relaxes other people. And then he strikes.

"So what you guarding?" he asks me.

"A little jewelry store on Hill," I say.

"You got a gun?" he says.

"Don't need one," I say. "It's pretty quiet."

I don't tell him I'm not allowed to carry because of my record. We aren't friends yet. Some of these youngsters, first thing out of their mouths is their crimes and their times. They've got no shame at all.

"What you gonna do if some motherfucker comes in waving a gat, wanting to take the place down?" Leon says.

I sip my beer and shrug. "Ain't my store," I say. "I'll be ducking and covering."

"Listen at him," Leon hoots. "Ducking and covering. My man be ducking and covering."

The smoke hanging in the air is starting to get to me. The music pulses in my fingertips, and my grin turns goofy. I'm looking right at the girls now, not even trying to be sly about it. The little one's titty is about to fall out of her blouse.

Leon's voice comes to me from a long way off. "I like you, man," he says. "You all right."

Satan's a sweet talker. I shake the fog from my head and down the rest of my beer. If you're a weak man, you better at least be smart enough to know when to walk away. I thank them for the drink, then hurry to my room. With the TV up loud, I can't hear the music, and pretty soon it gets back to being just like any other night.

EXCEPT THAT **I** DREAM about those girls. Dreams like I haven't dreamed in years. Wild dreams. Teenage dreams. And when I wake up humping nothing but the sheets, the disappointment almost does me in.

The darkness is a dead weight on my chest, and the hot air is like trying to breathe tar. My mind spins itself stupid, names ringing out, faces flying past. The little girl who'd lift her dress for us when we were eight or nine and show us what she got. My junior high and high school finger bangs and fumble fucks. Monique Carter and Shawnita Weber and that one that didn't wear panties because she didn't like how they looked under her skirt. Sharon, the mother of one of my kids, and Queenie, the mother of the other. All the whores I was with when I was stationed in Germany and all the whores I've been with since.

The right woman can work miracles. I've seen beasts tamed and crooked made straight. But in order for that to happen, you have to be the right man, and I've never been anybody's idea of right.

WE CLOSE FROM ONE to two for lunch, and I walk over and eat a cheeseburger at the same joint every afternoon. Then I go back to the store, the old man buzzes me in, and I flip the sign on the door to OPEN. Today the showroom smells like Windex when I return. Mr. M's been cleaning. I sit in my chair and close my eyes. It was a slow morning—one Mexican couple, a buck-toothed kid and a pregnant girl looking at wedding rings—and it's going to be a slow afternoon. The days fly by, but the hours drag on forever.

Around 3:30 someone hits the "Press For Entry" button outside. The chime goes off loud as hell, goosing me to my feet. Peering through the window, I see a couple of girls. I don't recognize them until the old man has already buzzed them in. It's the two from the other night, from the party in J Bone's room. They walk right past me, and if they see who I am, they don't show it.

Mr. M asks can he help them. "Let me look at this," they say, "Let me look at that," and while the old man is busy inside the case, their eyes roam the store. I realize they aren't interested in any watches or gold chains. They're making maps, scoping out the cameras and trying to peek into the back room.

I look out the window again, and there's Leon standing on the curb with J Bone and Dallas. They've got their backs to me, but I know Leon's suit and Bone's restless shuffle. Leon throws a glance over his shoulder at the store, can't resist. There's no way he can see me through the reflections on the glass, but I duck just the same.

I go back and stand next to my chair. I cross my arms over my chest and stare up at the clock on the wall. There's a way of being in prison, of making yourself invisible while still holding down your place. I feel like I'm on the yard again or in line for chow. You walk out that gate, but you're never free. What your time has taught you is a chain that hobbles you for the rest of your days.

The girls put on a show, something about being late to meet somebody. They're easing their way out.

"I could go $375 on this," the old man says, holding up a bracelet.

"We're gonna keep looking," they say.

"$350."

"Not today."

The old man sighs as they head for the door, puts the bracelet back in the case. Every lost sale stings him like his first. The girls walk past me, again without a glance or nod, anything that a cop studying a tape might spot. The heat rushes in when the door opens but is quickly gobbled up by the air conditioning, and the store is even quieter than it was before the girls came in.

I don't look at Mr. M because I'm afraid he'll see how worried I am. I sit in my chair like I normally do, stare at the floor like always. The girls are right now telling Leon what they saw, how easy it would be, and J Bone is saying, "We should do it today, nigga, nobody but the old man and McGruff in there, and him with no gun."

But Leon is smarter than that. "That ain't how we planned it," he says. "We're gonna take our time and do it right."

Him sending those girls in to case the store doesn't bode well for me. There's no way he didn't think I wouldn't remember them, which means he didn't care if I did. He either figures I won't talk afterward or, more likely, that I won't be able to.

THERE ARE LOTS OF Leons out there. The first one I ever met was named Malcolm, after Malcolm X. He was 12, a year younger than me, but acted 15 or 16. He was already into girls, into clothes, into making sure his hair was just right. I'd see him shooting craps with the older boys. I'd see him smoking Kools. The first time he spoke to me, I was like, "What's this slick motherfucker want with a broke-ass fool like me?" I was living in a foster home then, wearing hand-me down hand-me-downs, and the growling of my empty stomach kept me awake at night.

Malcolm's thing was shoplifting, and he taught me how. We started out taking candy from the Korean store, the two of us together, but after a while he had me in supermarkets, boosting laundry detergent and disposable razors and batteries while he waited outside. Then this junky named Maria would return the stuff to another store, saying she'd lost the receipt. We'd hit a few different places a day and split the money three ways. I never questioned why Maria and I were doing Malcolm's dirty work, I was just happy to have him as a friend. Old men called this kid sir, and the police let him be. It was like I'd lived in the dark before I met him.

The problem was, every few years after that a new Malcolm came along, and pretty soon I'd find myself in the middle of some shit I shouldn't have been in the middle of, trying to impress him. "You know what's wrong with you?" Queenie, the mother of my son once said. She always claimed to have me figured out. "You think you can follow someone to get somewhere, but don't nobody you know know where the hell they're going either."

She was right about that. In fact, the last flashy bastard who got past my good sense talked me right into prison, two years in Lancaster. I was a 33-year-old man about to get fired from Popeye's Chicken for mouthing off to my 20-year-old boss. "That's ridiculous," Kay Jay said. "You're better than that." He had a friend who ran a chop shop, he said. Dude had a shopping list of cars he'd pay for.

"Yeah, but I'm trying to stay out of trouble," I said.

"This ain't trouble," Kay Jay said. "This is easy money."

I ended up going down for the second car I stole. The police lit me up before I'd driven half a block, and I never heard from Kay Jay again, not a "Tough luck, bro," nothing. It took that to teach me my lesson. I can joke about it now and say I was a slow learner, but it still hurts to think I was so stupid for so long.

WHEN THE HEAT BREAKS late in the day, folks crawl out of their sweatboxes and drag themselves down to the street to get some fresh air and let the breeze cool their skin. They sit on the sidewalk with their backs to a wall or stand on busy corners and tell each other jokes while passing a bottle. The dope dealers work the crowd, signaling with winks and whistles, along with the Mexican woman who peddles T-shirts and tube socks out of a shopping cart and a kid trying to sell a phone that he swears up and down is legit.

I usually enjoy walking through the bustle, a man who's done a day of work and earned a night of rest. I like seeing the easy light of the setting sun on people's faces and hearing them laugh. Folks call out to me and shake my hand as I pass by, and there's an old man who plays the trumpet like you've never heard anyone play the trumpet for pocket change.

I barrel past it all today, not even pausing to drop a quarter in the old man's case. My mind is knotted around one worry: what I'm gonna say to Leon. I haven't settled on anything by the time I see him and his boys standing in front of the hotel, so it won't be a pretty speech, just the truth.

The three of them are puffing on cigars, squinting against the smoke as I roll up.

"Evening, fellas," I say.

"What up, officer," J Bone drawls.

Dallas giggles at his foolishness, but Leon doesn't crack a smile. The boy's already got a stain on his suit, on the lapel of the coat. He blows a smoke ring and looks down his nose at me.

"I saw them girls in the store today," I say to him.

"They was doing some shopping," he says.

"I saw you all too."

"We was waiting on them."

He's been drinking. His eyes are red and yellow, and his breath stinks. I get right to my point.

"Ain't nothing in there worth losing your freedom for," I say.

"What are you talking about?" Leon says.

"Come on, man, I been around," I say.

"He been around," Bone says, giggling again.

"You've got an imagination, I'll give you that," Leon says.

"I hope that's all it is," I say.

Leon steps up so he's right in my face. We're not two inches apart, and the electricity coming off him makes the hair on my arms stand up.

"Are you fucking crazy?" he says.

"Maybe so," I mumble, and turn to go. When I'm about to pull open the lobby door, he calls after me.

"How much that old man pay you?"

"He pays me what he pays me," I say.

"I was wondering, 'cause you act like you the owner."

"I'm just looking out for my own ass."

Leon smiles, trying to get back to being charming. With his kind, though, once you've seen them without their masks, it's never the same.

"And you know the best way to do that, right?" he says.

"Huh?" I say.

"Duck and cover," he says.

He's going to shoot me dead. I hear it in his voice. He's already got his mind made up.

YOUNGBLOOD SAYS HE KNOWS someone who can get me a gun, a white boy named Paul, a gambler, a loser, one of them who's always selling something. I tell Youngblood I'll give him twenty to set something up. Youngblood calls the guy, and the guy says he has a little .25 auto he wants a hundred bucks for. That's fine, I say. I have three hundred hidden in my room. It's supposed to be Mexico money, but there isn't going to be any Mexico if Leon puts a bullet in me.

Paul wants to meet on Sixth and San Pedro at 9pm. It's a long walk over, and Youngblood talks the whole way there about his usual nothing. He has to stop three times. Once to piss and twice to ask some shaky-looking brothers where's a dude named Cisco. I'm glad I have my money in my sock. I don't like to dawdle after dark. They'll cut you for a quarter down here, for half a can of beer.

We're a few minutes late to the corner, but this Paul acts like it was an hour. "What the fuck?" he keeps saying, "What the fuck?" looking up and down the street like he expects the police to pop out any second. He has a bandage over one eye and is wearing a T-shirt with cartoon racehorses on it, the kind they give away at the track sometimes.

"Show me what you got," I say, interrupting his complaining.

"Show you what I got?" he says. "Show me what you got."

I reach into my sock and bring out the roll of five twenties. I hand it to him, and he thumbs quickly through the bills.

"Wait here," he says.

"Hold on now," I say.

"It's in my car," he says. "You motherfuckers may walk around with guns on you, but I don't."

He hurries off toward a beat-up Nissan parked in a loading zone.

"It's cool," Youngblood says. "Relax."

Paul opens the door of the car and gets in. He starts the engine, revs it, then drives away. I stand there with my mouth open, wondering if I misunderstood him, that he meant he was going somewhere else to get the gun and then bring it back. But that isn't what he said. Thirty years on the street, and I haven't learned a goddamn thing. I hit Youngblood so hard, his eyes roll up in his head. Then I kick him when he falls, leave him whining like a whipped puppy.

I DON'T SLEEP THAT NIGHT or the next, and at work I can't sit still, waiting for what's coming. Two days pass, three, four. At the hotel, I see Leon hanging around the lobby and partying in J Bone's room. We don't say anything to each other as I pass by, I don't even look at him, but our souls scrape like ship's hulls, and I shudder from stem to stern.

When Friday rolls around and still nothing has happened, I start to think I'm wrong. Maybe what I said to Leon was enough to back him off. Maybe he was never serious about robbing the store. My load feels a little lighter. For the first time in a week I can twist my head without the bones in my neck popping.

To celebrate, I take myself to Denny's for dinner. Chicken fried steak and mashed potatoes. A big Mexican family is there celebrating something. Looks like Mom and Dad and Grandma and a bunch of kids, everyone all dressed up. I'm 42 years old, not young anymore, but I'd still like to have something like that someday. Cancer took my daughter when she was 10, and my son's stuck in prison. If I ever make it to Mexico, maybe I'll get a second chance, and this time, it would mean something.

They show up at 2:15 on Saturday. We've just reopened after lunch, and I haven't even settled into my chair yet when the three of them crowd into the doorway. Dallas is in front, a hoodie pulled low over his face. He's the one who pushes the buzzer, the one Leon's got doing the dirty work.

"Don't let 'em in," I shout to Mr. M.

The old man toddles in from the back room, confused.

"What?"

"Don't touch the buzzer."

Dallas rings again, then raps on the glass with his knuckles. I've been afraid for my life before—on the street, in prison, in rooms crowded with men not much more than animals—but it's not something you get used to. My legs shake like they have every other time I've been sure death is near, and my heart tries to tear itself loose and run away. I crouch, get up, then crouch again, a chicken with its head cut off.

J Bone tugs a ski mask down over his face and pushes Dallas out of the way. He charges the door, slamming into it shoulder-first, which makes a hell of a noise, but that's about it. He backs up, tries again, then lifts his foot and drives his heel into the thick, bulletproof glass a couple of times. The door doesn't budge.

"I'm calling the police," the old man shouts at him. "I've already pressed the alarm."

Leon yells at Bone, and Bone yells at Leon, but I can't hear what they're saying. Leon has his mask pulled down now too. He draws a gun from his pocket, and I scramble for cover behind a display case as he fires two rounds into the lock. He doesn't understand the mechanics, the bolts that shoot into steel and concrete above and below when you turn the key.

People on the street are stopping to see what's going on. Dallas runs off, followed by Bone. Leon grabs the door handle and yanks on it, then gives up too. He peels off his mask and starts to walk one way before turning quickly and jogging in the other.

I get up and go to the door to make sure they're gone for real.

I should be relieved, but I'm not. I'm already worried about what's going to happen next.

"Those black bastards," Mr. M says. "Those fucking black bastards."

ONCE THEY FIND OUT about my record, the police get in their head that we were all in it together and it's just that I lost my nerve at the last minute.

"How did you know not to let them in?" they ask me twenty different times in twenty different ways.

"I saw the gun," I say, simple as that.

Mr. M ends up going to the hospital with chest pains, and his son shows up to square everything away. He keeps thanking me for protecting his father.

"You may have saved his life," he says, and I wish I could say that's who I was thinking about.

The police don't finish investigating until after six. I hang around the store until then because I'm not ready to go back to the hotel. When the cops finally pack up, I walk home slowly, all the way there expecting Leon to come out of nowhere like a lightning bolt. There'll be a gun in his hand, or a knife. He knows how it goes: If you're worried about a snitch, take him out before he talks.

I make it back safely, though. Leon's not waiting out front or in the lobby or on the stairs. The door to J Bone's room is open, but no music is playing, and nobody's laughing. I glance in, and see that the room is empty except for a bunch of greasy burger bags and half-finished 40's with cigarettes sunk in them.

I lock my door when I get inside my room, open the window, turn on the fan. My legs stop working, and I collapse on the bed, exhausted. I dig out a bottle of Ten High that I keep for when the demons come dancing and decide that if I make it through tonight, I'll treat every hour I have left as a gift.

I **TALK TO THE CHINAMAN** at the desk the next morning, and he tells me J Bone checked out yesterday, ran off in a hurry. Youngblood is listening in, pretending to watch the lobby TV. We haven't spoken since I lost my temper.

"What do you know about it?" I call to him, not sure if he'll answer.

"Cost you five dollars to find out," he says.

I hand over the money, and he jumps up off the couch, eager to share. He says Leon and Bone had words yesterday afternoon, talking about the police being after them and "You stupid," "No, you stupid." Next thing they went upstairs, came down with their shit, and split.

"What do you think they did?" Youngblood asks me.

"Fuck if I know," I say. "Ask your friend Paul."

"He ain't my friend," Youngblood says. "I put the word out on him. I'm gonna get you your money back."

I'm so happy to have Leon gone that I don't even care about the money. I ask Youngblood if he wants to go for breakfast. He's a good kid. A couple of hours from now, after he takes his first shot, he'll be useless, but right now I can see the little boy he once was in his crooked smile.

He talks about Kobe—Kobe this, Kobe that—as we walk to McDonalds. We go back and forth from shady patches still cool as night to blocks that even this early are being scorched by the sun. Nobody's getting crazy yet, and it doesn't smell too bad except in the alleys. Almost like morning anywhere. I keep looking over my shoulder, but I can feel myself relaxing already. A couple more days, and I'll be back to normal.

MR. **M'S SON TOLD** me before I left the store that it'd be closed for at least a week, but not to worry because they'd pay me like I was still working. The next Thursday he calls and asks me to come down. The old man is still in the hospital, and it doesn't look like he'll be getting out anytime soon, so the son has decided to shut the store up for good. He hands me an envelope with $2,500 inside, calls it severance.

"Thank you again for taking care of my father," he says.

"Tell him I said hello and get well soon," I reply.

The next minute I'm out on the street, unemployed for the first time in years. I have to laugh. I barely gave Leon the time of day, didn't fall for his mess, didn't jump when he said to, and he still managed to fuck up the good thing I had going. That's the way it is. Every time you manage to stack a few bricks, a wave's bound to come along and knock them down.

THEY RUN GIRLS OUT of vans over on Towne. You pay a little more than you would for a street whore, but they're generally younger and cleaner, and doing it in the van is better than doing it behind a dumpster or in an Andy Gump. I shower and shave before I head out, get a hundred bucks from my stash behind the light switch and stick it in my sock.

Mama-san is carrying more groceries up the stairs, both kids hanging on her as I'm going down.

"No cooking," I say. "No cooking."

She doesn't reply, but the kids look scared. I didn't mean for that to happen.

The freaks come out at night, and the farther east you go, the worse it gets. Sidewalk shitters living in cardboard boxes, ghosts who eat out of garbage cans, a blind man showing his dick on the corner. I keep my gaze forward, my hands balled into fists. Walking hard, we used to call it.

Three vans are parked at the curb tonight. I make a first pass to scope out the setup. The pimps stand together, a trio of cocky little vatos with gold chains and shiny shirts. My second time by, they start in hissing through their teeth and whispering, "Big tits, tight pussy."

"You looking for a party?" one of them asks me.

"What if I am?" I say.

He walks me to his van and slides open the side door. I smell weed and something coconut. A chubby Mexican girl wearing a red bra and panties is lying on a mattress back there. She's pretty enough, for a whore, but I'd still like to check out what's in the other vans. I don't want to raise a ruckus though.

"How much," I say to nobody in particular.

The pimp says forty for head, a hundred for half and half. I get him down to eighty. I crawl inside the van, and he closes the door behind me. There's cardboard taped to the windshield and windows. The only light is what seeps in around the edges. I'm sweating already, big drops racing down my chest inside my shirt.

"How you doing tonight?" I say to the girl.

"Okay," she says.

She uses her hand to get me hard, then slips the rubber on with her mouth. I make her stop after just a few seconds and have her lay back on the mattress. I come as soon as I stick it in. It's been a long time.

"Can I lay here a minute?" I say.

The girl shrugs and cleans herself with a baby wipe. She has nice hair, long and black, and big brown eyes. I ask her where she's from. She says Mexico.

"I'm moving down there someday," I say.

My mouth gets away from me. I tell her I was in Germany once, when I was in the Army, and that I came back and had two kids. I tell her about leaving them just like my mom and dad left me, and how you say you're never going to do certain things, but then you do. I tell her that's why God's turned away from us and Jesus is a joke. When I run out of words, I'm crying. The tears get mixed up with the sweat on my face.

"It's okay," the girl says. "It's okay."

Her pimp bangs on the side of the van and opens the door. Time's up.

I'VE SEEN ENOUGH THAT I could write my own Bible. For example, here's the parable of the brother who hung on and the one who fell: Two months later I'm walking home from my new job guarding a Mexican dollar store on Los Angeles. A bum steps out in front of me, shoves his dirty hand in my face and asks for a buck. I don't like when they're pushy, and I'm about to tell him to step off, but then I realize it's Leon.

He's still wearing his suit, only now it's filthy rags. His eyes are dull and overcast, his lips burnt black from the pipe. All his charm is gone, all his "kiss my ass" cockiness. Nobody is following this boy anymore but the reaper.

"Leon?" I say. I'm not scared of him. One punch now would turn him back to dust.

"Who you?" he asks, warily.

"You don't remember?"

He opens his eyes wide, then squints. A quiet laugh rattles his bones.

"Old McGruff," he says. "Gimme a dollar, crime dog."

I give him two.

"Be good to yourself," I say as I walk away.

"You're a lucky man," he calls after me.

No, I'm not, but I am careful. Got a couple bricks stacked, a couple bucks put away, and one eye watching for the next wave. Forever and ever, amen.

LIPSTICK AND HANDCUFFS

MICHAEL HEMMINGSON

ANNIE AND **I** WERE walking along the beach and we saw the body. At first we thought it was someone lying on the sand, sleeping. We weren't sure if it was a man or woman. This person had long stringy blond hair and wore baggy jeans. It looked like this person was wearing thick red lipstick. We changed our path to walk around the person. Annie said, Something isn't right. She said, Hank, something is wrong.

The person was a man, and the man had lipstick smeared on his lips and make-up caked on his cheeks and forehead, like someone had tried to paint him up as a clown. His hands were handcuffed behind his back and his eyes stared upwards. He was not blinking. He was not moving.

Is he dead? Annie said.

I let go of her hand and stepped toward the man, my feet sinking into the sand.

Annie said, Don't go near him!

I just need to look, I said.

Please don't, she said.

I had to have a closer look. Flies swarmed around the body. The guy was not breathing. He appeared dead but I had never seen a dead body.

Annie grabbed my hand and pulled me back. She said, Let's get out of here.

I think he's dead.

It's none of our business, she said.

What should we do?

We should get away from here, she said.

We need to tell someone, I said.

Why?

The police, I said, we should call the police.

Why? Someone else will see the body. Why does it have to be us?

We have to, I said.

No one has to do anything, Hank.

Annie wanted to walk fast. She was pulling me with her.

We found a lifeguard on a three-wheel ATV. I told him about the body. Annie was not happy. The lifeguard acted like he didn't believe us.

It was in the news the next day, on TV and in the papers: two unnamed teenagers find a dead body on the beach. No mention of the make-up, lipstick and handcuffs. The man, said the news, was unidentified, said the police. A detective came by my parents' house asking a few questions. Annie was there in my room, we had been kissing and touching but she was distant. We were both still virgins. She was having nightmares about the dead body. The detective didn't ask much, just what time did we find the body, did we notice anyone suspicious, did we touch the body.

I wish we never took that walk, Annie said.

Two days later, when we were alone, Annie and I lost our virginities to one another. She said it was time because she could die any day and she didn't want to die not knowing what sex was all about. It was quick, sticky and smelly. Annie cried after. She said, What if I'm pregnant now?

She was not pregnant, not that time or many times after. But eventually she was, and we went to get an abortion at a feminist clinic that didn't ask too many questions.

Annie cried for the loss. We're murderers now, she said.

We were one month away from graduating high school.

She still had nightmares about the dead body. Annie said, His eyes—I always see his eyes, and the handcuffs and lipstick.

The body was identified. His name was Max Spiers, a resident of Colorado, many states away. He was a known associate of drug dealers. There were no leads in the case, no suspects.

What if those drug dealers come looking for us? Annie said.

Why would they? I said.

Because we found the body, she said.

We didn't see anything, I said.

We saw enough.

We graduated and didn't know what to do with ourselves. Annie considered nursing school because the government offered grants. My parents were not happy that I didn't get a scholarship to a nice college. I didn't try, that was the problem.

Annie wanted to go to church so we could be forgiven for our sins. We killed a baby, she said, and Jesus is not happy.

Jesus, I said.

But I went to a Baptist church with her. There was a lot of talk about sin, blood, and the pain Jesus felt when big nails were hammered into his hands and feet.

He suffered for your sins, said the pastor.

Annie cried. She said, It isn't fair Jesus should feel the pain for something we did.

She looked at the nine-foot Jesus on the church wall: eyes cast upward, blood flowing from the head, hands and feet.

A week later she gave her life to the statue. I was not with her when she did this. She said we couldn't have sex anymore until we got married. We were still seventeen and I had no intention of getting married or having children for quite a while. She demanded that I become born again with her. I said no. She said, I can't be with you if you are not like me.

She broke up with me. I joined the army when I turned eighteen two months later. My parents did not like that.

A year later, I was stationed at Fort Dix and Iraq invaded Kuwait. I was sent there with my company. In Iraq, I saw lots of dead bodies with eyes staring at nothing.

Five years later, I was in a grocery store and Annie was working behind a register.

I heard you went to the war, she said.

Yes, I said.

You came back unharmed, she said.

I'm alive, I said.

I didn't bother to tell her about the problems I had with my lungs. I was breathing some bad stuff in those burning oil fields.

Look at me, she said, turning to her side. She had a pregnant belly. Five months, she said.

Who is the dad?

She didn't say. I was glad to get away from her. I never went back to that grocery store. I heard the father was some guy at the church who had a drug problem and was in prison. I heard she gave the baby up for adoption.

I moved to Alaska.

Four years later, Annie sent me a letter through my parents telling me that the cold case of the murder of Max Spiers was solved. Some drug runner confessed to all his crimes as part of a plea deal in federal court to not get the death sentence for the murder of a woman and her baby. The drug runner was from

South Carolina. She sent me newspaper clippings. When asked why Max Spiers had on lipstick and handcuffs, the killer said, He was a bitch snitch and looked better that way.

In the letter, Annie asked why I moved to Alaska, was I married, was I going to go to our high school reunion. She wrote she was married and had two children now, both girls. She wrote she had a son somewhere out there with a good Christian family.

I did not go to the high school reunion. I returned home when my father died. My mother died not long after. I moved into the house I grew up in. I went to church every Sunday.

I went to the fifteen-year high school reunion. Annie was not there. Someone told me her husband molested one of her daughters and she stabbed him with a knife. He did not die and she was not charged.

I got married to a woman nine years my junior. She was a good woman I met at church. We had three kids.

Annie found me on Facebook. It had been twenty years since we'd seen each other. You look the same as you did when you were seventeen, she wrote about my Facebook photo.

She did not. She had gained fifty pounds and had many lines on her face. She told me she was a grandmother now.

Do you ever think about the beach and that body? she asked.

No, I replied.

I still have nightmares, she told me.

We talked on the phone. I asked her if she was going to attend the twenty-five year reunion. She said she was living in Arkansas and didn't have the money, didn't want people to see her fat and old. It was so long ago, she wrote. I'm not the same person I used to be, she said.

Jesus loves you as you are, I said.

Jesus, she said.

HEAD

DARRIN DOYLE

THE HUSBAND'S HEAD STOPPED.

No trauma. No pain. No warning. On the phone, in the middle of explaining to a woman from Duluth that her policy did not cover any act of God involving water, and therefore, regrettably, she would not receive Prime Way compensation, the husband's words were snuffed out like candles in space.

He fell into blackness. All sound sucked away. He was aware of the physical world, but from a distance, as if he had plunged into a deep hole. He no longer conceived of either his hand or the receiver; he only sensed a distant part of himself—like an old, half-forgotten memory—that stood in contact with an object, and that object should be used for destruction.

On the surface, he roared into violence.

Two colleagues subdued the husband when he began hitting his computer monitor with the phone. While they wrestled him to the floor, they noticed how his head drooped like a flower with a broken stem. Saliva spilled from his mouth. They wondered if he was dying, and privately imagined taking his vacated cubicle.

The coworkers resented the husband, not only because his desk stood nearest the restroom. He never took sick days. He was always on time. For more than ten years, he'd skipped the Monday doughnuts. He was supremely disciplined or supremely spineless. Either way, they hated him for making them into slobs.

Paramedics rushed the husband to the hospital. Neurologists applied non-invasive tests for two hours, after which they declared his head "no longer viable."

Bedside, they pronounced the diagnosis. The patient didn't hear. Engulfed in blackness, he only felt a queasy, off-pitch drone signaling that his essence was motionless, rootless, and cosmically out-of-touch.

He bucked and flailed and tore at the doctors' shirts.

Burly staffers situated the husband under heavy straps and inserted a pillow behind his head. The nurses frowned at him. "Such a tragedy," one said. "Still got most of his hair," said the other. She clucked her tongue at the Rolex on his bedside table. "You can't take it with you," the other one agreed.

THE HOSPITAL NOTIFIED THE wife, who left her yoga class to be with him. She stroked the husband's chest and held his hand. He lay with his face toward her, his blue eyes wooden. It was unnerving, this deserted stare. His bloodless cheeks appeared deflated, or perhaps this was an effect of the milky light filtering through the curtains.

It had been weeks, the wife realized, since she'd bothered to really *see* him. He'd become a collection of parts and impressions:

a mouth, an arm, dirty socks, Barbasol. Studying him now, he scarcely resembled the man she'd married. This thing on the bed was a sculptor's rendition, a mannequin.

The lining of the wife's skirt caused her knees to itch. A chill rode her body. The diagnosis made no sense. Was this a joke?

She thought she should get a second opinion. But if the second doctor said it was just a concussion, wouldn't she automatically believe it? It was human nature to cling to the more palatable answer. And in the end, wouldn't the palatable diagnosis be wrong? Wouldn't the husband die? Wouldn't she be hobbled by guilt forever? Wouldn't their daughter feel resentful? And years later, becoming a mother herself, wouldn't the daughter resent her own daughter for making her feel guilty about having resented her mother?

Even under ordinary circumstances, such questions often plagued the wife. She dreaded mistakes, although normally her fears involved off-brand toilet paper or pondering a salon visit after reading about an Alabama woman who contracted leprosy during a pedicure.

Her hippie parents had raised her to be skeptical of authority figures, and even though the wife wasn't a hippie and in fact resented her parents' anti-establishmentarianism and New Age spirituality, she had always embraced the inquisitive impulse. Lately, questioning felt like a euphemism for self-doubt.

She decided not to get a second opinion.

The husband stared. His chest rose and fell.

Gazing into his lusterless eyes, she felt certain that she loved him. Yes, he had flaws: his collection of internet porn; his unwillingness to discipline their teenage daughter; his obsession with the Vietnam War (which had claimed his father's life); his middle-age flab; his foot fungus; his devotion to Prime Way.

But why go on? Nobody was perfect. People were more than lists, right? Line up the good over here, the bad over there, see which side is longer, and there's your verdict? Ridiculous.

Choking on the stench of isopropyl alcohol, the wife craved a cigarette. She pictured herself lighting one and pulling a long drag—her first in, what, two decades? She needed the distraction.

"You're the experts," she said to the neurologists by the window. For ten minutes they'd been studying her from behind clipboards. "But if his head is," she struggled for the right word, "a vegetable, then why is he breathing? Why do his hands move?"

The younger doctor chuckled. "No one said 'vegetable.' We said 'no longer viable.'"

"But why is his body moving?" said the wife.

"Have you ever seen a chicken without a head?" the young doctor asked. "It has all kinds of moves. In Ohio, 1993, a farmer chopped off a chicken's head, but the chicken survived. They stuffed bits of apple into its neckhole for forty days before it died."

"Your husband's condition is unusual, but not unheard of," said the older doctor. "There was a case in Mexico in the '70s. Or was it Beirut in the '80s?" He looked to his colleague, who pursed his lips and said nothing. "The good news is that your husband's motor functions are completely normal. He can stand, walk, run. He could tap dance on a tennis court if he was into that sort of thing. Theoretically, of course. I mean, he's physically capable of it. Whether or not he does it, that's another issue, and I wouldn't get your hopes up. His lungs are drawing air, so he won't die. Nutrition isn't a problem as he is still able to swallow liquids. But he can't chew. Nor can he be trained to chew. In many ways, however, he's still the man you married."

"Think of the head as another appendage. A glorified arm."

The wife was about to say she didn't marry him for conversations with his arm, but a nurse sidled up to the other side of the bed and inserted a tube between the husband's lips. By squeezing a translucent sack, the nurse sent clay-colored paste into his throat. The husband's throat convulsed. Now and then she repositioned his face so the tube remained intact.

The wife couldn't stop picturing her husband doing a theoretical tap dance on a tennis court. "Don't you mean his *brain* isn't viable?" she said.

"Head. We mean head," the young doctor answered. "Squeeze his cheek."

When the wife hesitated, the young doctor reached across her and administered an aggressive pinch. The husband's skin reddened, but he gave no response.

"The entire head is without feeling," he continued. "Not only the brain."

"The bigger question is this," the gray-haired doctor interrupted. "Do you want to leave the head intact?"

"He no longer needs it." The young doctor's tone suggested they were discussing the fate of a shabby baseball cap.

The wife returned the young doctor's gaze without feeling. She wanted him to witness, displayed on her own face, his profound insignificance. He was aware of his good looks, which annoyed her. Early thirties, she guessed, bleached teeth, forehead tall as a billboard. Hotshot. Always got what he wanted. Graduated med school by twenty-two. Swarthy eyebrows the color of her husband's shoulder mole. Every click of his pen was an attitude.

The older doctor cleared his throat. "His head will become unsightly in the coming weeks," he said, fingering his wattle in a way that made the wife sad. "It's not necrotic yet, but blood flow has dramatically decreased. All that bobbing will stress the neck."

The young doctor described the amputation procedure. His accent was Greek—or Turkish?—his hands fluttering like birds as he spoke. Distracted by his pantomime, the wife caught only random phrases: "Fourth and fifth vertebrae"; "donate to science"; "purely cosmetic"; "minimal scarring, easily hidden."

The young doctor slid a brochure into her fist. His complicated odor filled her nose. She said she would think about it.

THE HUSBAND WAS TO be discharged the next day.

He demonstrated the ability to walk, grab, hold, and kick. He could push buttons on the hospital remote, but he did so without purpose and pressed so forcefully that the plastic cracked. He voided his bowels wherever it happened, in part because he couldn't see, hear, or speak. He didn't seem to understand where, or what, he was, or even what a "what" or "where" was. He was a 224-pound pastrami sandwich.

"Can he think?" The wife signed the release form. "Will he know me or our daughter?"

"All doubtful," the young doctor said with a lusty smile, his pheromones filling a balloon between them, jostling her, bumping her. "His head is literally a pile of macaroni." He read the MRI results and slid a hand around her waist, giving a squeeze.

"I see what you mean," the wife said. Her face heated. The neurologist was an idiot; he used "literally" in literally the wrong way. He was an inch shorter, fifteen years younger. And she wasn't pushing him away.

Now she was home with her husband, who staggered, lurched, and bulldozed. He toppled lamps and collided with walls. She placed a bottle of beer into his hand, his favorite, St. Pauli Girl. He poured it onto his lap and the rest of the world. He'd become a collection of reflexes, a machine. Before, he'd at least been a machine that could dress itself.

His destructiveness transcended slapstick. Objects in his reach became crushed or weapons or both. All the Hummel figurines inherited from his mother exploded against the ceiling. Burst bananas spilled their guts over his fingers. His null stare never changed. His head was a bell clapper.

The wife retreated to a corner, transfixed. The slamming of her heart wasn't from fear; she knew, without any evidence that she could articulate, that her husband wouldn't hurt her. What she felt was awe. He was more energetic than she'd ever seen.

He'd never been violent. All of his successes had come from a measured persistence and lapdog charm he wasn't even aware he possessed.

She kept thinking of the doctor's words: "In many ways, he's still the man you married."

She couldn't decide if this was true. Yes, he was still distant and uncommunicative. Yes, he didn't ask about her day or help with the dishes.

But now he had a fire inside. His passion was directionless, untamed, and on display. He wasn't siphoning himself into that goddamn Vietnam book, hunched over a keyboard in the dark.

And now he liked to be touched. Her hand on his knee, fingertip on his back, toe on his foot, any contact, and he settled. He stilled.

The husband had never stilled. He'd worked eleven-hour days, taken meals in front of the TV, typed on the computer until midnight, read in bed until she forced him to kill the lamp. While asleep, he even mumbled about the NFL draft and revision deadlines for debris removal clauses.

THE WIFE TIED THE husband to the recliner with nylon rope. This was in order to cook, go to bed, take a shower, drive their fifteen-year-old to school, and so on.

The wife brought the daughter into the living room so she could see the husband struggling against his restraints. The wife only wanted to frighten the daughter a little. She wanted the daughter to understand that this was serious.

The daughter frowned and scrolled through her text messages. She hadn't been close to her father, emotionally, since he had taught her to fly a kite. So while the sight of his limp head was upsetting (the daughter's eyes glistened with tears... unless... was she high?), the daughter apparently viewed the current medical trauma as an issue that had nothing to do with her.

"I get it, Mom. It's serious. *Life* is serious. I'm bloated, and I've got a huge Econ test I haven't studied for."

"Okay. But this is more serious. Take your serious and multiply it. Here. Here's a calculator. Multiply it."

In the following days, the daughter's attitude worsened. "You say it's tragic," she said over Quaker Oats, "but he's alive, isn't he?" She nodded at the husband, who was duct-taped to the kitchen chair. "I needed to be fed when I was a baby. Was I a medical emergency? God, Mom."

The daughter continued, her words rapid-fire (didn't meth do that to a person?) "In fact, he's more present now than ever. And don't you want to be a part of it? Don't you want to repay him for all those years he worked so you could paint nude models and do Pilates? He's *here*. Isn't this what you've wanted?"

The outburst caught the wife off-guard. The daughter's normal mode of communication consisted of sighs and sardonic chortles. The wife whipped up a succinct response: "It's not your place to tell me what I want. Let's not forget who's boss."

The daughter acted as if she hadn't heard. "Isn't this so-called 'crisis' actually a miracle? This isn't a health emergency, Mom. It's a karmic imperative."

"A what? Where did you hear that phrase?"

The daughter stood and pointed at the husband. "*Karmic imperative*, Mom. To balance the cosmic scales and show this man we will not allow him to escape this body without achieving true intimacy!"

The wife leaned over the sink, staring into the drain. Her daughter's words echoed like a sick chorus—karma, cosmic scales, intimacy. It was true, then. Despite the wife's best efforts to live a disciplined, materialistic existence—a life of goals, competition, and earning, where goods weren't a badge of greed but a badge of merit that showed you were alive, you desired, you were self-sufficient and—God forbid—evolved... Despite these efforts, the granola gene had passed through her and into the child. The wife blamed herself. Who else could she blame? Her parents had been dead for ten years.

Maybe this was the husband's doing. All that Vietnam talk since their daughter was small. All those PBS specials and History Channel documentaries. Sure, the husband never said specifically that the war had been wrong and that his father had died for no reason. But the daughter had a brain. She'd seen footage.

And for all of his insurance acumen, the husband had never been a go-getter. He had served Prime Way for years yet was never offered the Regional Director position. He accepted his annual 2.5% raise and requested nothing more. This house, this life, was adequate, but it could have been nicer. The Websters had a Jacuzzi. The Clemenses had a 78-inch plasma and a landscaper.

The wife decided to take action.

She turned from the sink and faced her daughter. "I have a surprise. Today you can drive yourself to school in the new Cherokee."

"That's Dad's car."

"He's not going to need it."

"I don't have a license."

"A permit's the same damn thing. And here's a hundred bucks. Get yourself another tattoo."

PRIME WAY OFFERED GENEROUS disability, so the family was covered for a year—dependent, of course, on the wife's ability to convince HR over the telephone that the husband would return to work.

The HR rep was a stickler. She requested to speak with medical staff to confirm the non-chronic nature of the husband's condition. It wasn't difficult to find the young doctor.

"It's about time," he laughed over the phone. His presumptuousness both irked and excited the wife. He was challenging her beliefs, taunting her values.

What beliefs? What values? The wife didn't know. But he was taunting something, and it pleased her.

He had remained in her thoughts for the past two weeks. She'd begun to make him more beautiful than in real life. She gave him vital lashes; soft, hirsute hands; burnt-almond eyes aflame with need and compassion.

She envisioned her husband wearing the same gaze; the idea made her giggle at the counter while whirring chuck for his dinner. Her husband was one of those rare people who'd been born satisfied, and every day from infancy had rearranged itself to fulfill his birthright. He had never needed anyone. He was disgustingly self-reliant. He even took the central trauma of his life—his father's death in a POW camp—and turned it into a project, a book he would never complete because it was the process, he said, that healed him.

The paste in the blender reminded her of dog food.

That evening, at the wife's urging, the daughter went to the Clemenses to babysit. The doctor parked his black Audi in the driveway. The wife spent the evening with him. Every action of the young neurologist exceeded yet disappointed her expectation.

He cracked jokes. She didn't understand the punchlines. He dressed impeccably, looking rigid and striking in his gray wool jacket and mauve turtleneck. A smear of shaving cream decorated his Adam's apple. She ordered Chinese. He ate with a fork and burped into his hand. He selected a CD of classical waltzes, then pushed aside the coffee table and took her in his arms. His heel crushed her bare toes. After dancing, they drank merlot. She tickled him; he wasn't ticklish. They discussed movies and vegetables, neither of which he truly understood. He kissed her on the mouth for two minutes, and then, catching his breath, asked, "Where's your husband, by the way?"

"In the closet."

"May I see?" His wine-stained lips were blood clots.

They dragged the husband to the center of the living room.

His arms were crossed over his chest, bound like his ankles. His eyes were open.

"Fascinating." With a pen light from his jacket pocket, the young doctor illuminated the husband's eyes. "No response. And yet…" he paused before rearing back and punching the husband in the groin. "Watch." The husband convulsed; he writhed and strained; tendons bulged in his neck.

The wife was too stunned to speak. She smelled excrement. The husband had flooded his diapers.

"My point," said the young doctor, appearing not to notice the wife's tears, "is that we have always thought that cognitive function was necessary for pain. Or pleasure." He found the wife's hand and stroked it like a gerbil. He brought her close and embraced her, kissing her neck. "Perhaps we too can experience pleasure without our heads."

FOR THREE MONTHS, FLOWERS and cards arrived. Her husband was generally well-liked, but not specifically. The cards contained no personal messages. Visitors were rare: a co-worker; the daughter's art teacher; an uncle; a cousin. The husband's only immediate family was his brother, a corporate attorney who flew from Chicago on his own twin-engine with wife and four young sons in tow.

The brother insisted on untying the husband.

"Let me wrestle him," he said to the wife. He rolled up his shirtsleeves. "It'll jar his memory. We horsed around constantly when we were kids."

The match ended with the husband fracturing the brother's wrist. More damage would have been done if the eleven-year-old nephew hadn't leaped onto the husband's back and compelled him into a china hutch. The husband's right eyebrow was lacerated; an expensive vase shattered. The brother and his wife threatened legal action while walking out the door.

That evening, the young doctor peeled off the bandage to check the husband's eyebrow.

"I trust you were able to stop the bleeding," he asked.

The wife, on the couch, was attempting to repair the vase. She took a gulp of wine. "There was barely any blood. Do you have to do that while I'm sitting here?"

The young doctor was stitching the husband with needle and thread. The husband wriggled on the carpet. His bound hands were turning purple. "Hold still, bucko," the young doctor said. Then to the wife: "Come here and touch him so he stops moving."

"You're cutting off his circulation," the wife said. "I keep telling you, you tie him too tight. That's why he struggles. Do you have any heavy-duty medical glue at St. Mary's?"

"For your husband?"

"For the vase."

"Actually, yes. There's an epoxy for broken skulls. I'll bring home a tube. Why I didn't think of that!" He winked at her.

Home, he was calling it. Third time this week. The wife wasn't sure how to feel. Lately, she was having trouble knowing how to feel about many things: the laundry, her new deluxe mop head, her daughter's ennui, the stubborn cucumbers. The world was a soup—something creamed, through which she waded each day. She socked her husband's feet in the mornings and brushed his teeth at night. She swabbed him, shaved him, and changed his Depends. The young doctor worked eighty hours a week, slept with her when he could, and used their treadmill. The wife had taken up smoking. She rarely changed out of her sweat suit. Yoga, birdwatching, friends—these parts of her life had faded into memory.

"Oh, nuts," the young doctor said.

The wife glanced up from the shards in her lap.

The young doctor, cross-legged on the carpet, held forth his needle, which bore a skewered eyeball. The optic nerve and blood vessels dangled.

"It popped right out," the young doctor said.

"You did it on purpose. Are you pretending you didn't?"

"Let me get this straight. I took out his eyeball...why?"

"Don't patronize me. I'm not one of your chesty interns. I don't have lip gloss on my nipples, okay?"

"You worry me."

"Get in line."

"I don't understand."

"It means I worry myself. I thought you were a native speaker. You don't get the euphemisms, do you?"

"I never said native speaker. I said persuasive speaker."

"Did you lie about your past? From Cleveland, born and raised?"

"I can't be sure of what I said. I'm not a native speaker."

"Are you trying to bilk me out of my money? I'll burn down this house before anybody like you gets rich off it. He *designed* this house, okay?" She pointed at her one-eyed husband. "He didn't have any fancy architectural training. That's the kind of man he was. And now you have his eyeball on a pin..." She downed her wine and poured another glass.

"Your anger is healthy," the young doctor said. He set the eyeball on the coffee table and joined her on the couch. Gently, he folded the corners of her napkin over the vase shards. "Do this later, darling. Even God rested once a week."

She understood that he was talking about more than the vase. She had taken to repairing every object her husband had broken since his illness. For three months, reparations had been her top priority, at times neglecting to feed herself or her husband.

They heard the side door open and close. Sneakers squeaked through the kitchen and up the stairs.

"She's not adjusting," the wife said. "I signed over the Cherokee. She owns it. I bought her a new wardrobe—does she even care? I never thought I'd say it, but I wish my mom and dad were still around. She could live with them and see the alternative."

"Look at this," the young doctor said. He reached down, retrieved the pin, and brought the eyeball close to the wife's face.

She studied it. "The color isn't right."

"See how dark and flimsy these are?" He flicked the dangling fibers. "A healthy eyeball doesn't tear so easily. The lens, the receptors… shriveled like prunes. That eyebrow laceration should have bled rivers. Come with me."

Taking her hand, he pulled her down to the carpet, beside the husband.

"Compare the skin of the arm to the skin of the face."

"Yes," the wife said. The face was gray. She wondered if she had noticed but hadn't been able to acknowledge it.

"Soon, the head will be black. Then, the stench."

He showed her other things. The husband's sinuses and mouth had stopped producing moisture. His nostrils were inflamed and red. His tongue had swelled to twice its size. With a gentle tug, a clump of hair detached from the husband's scalp.

"Try the teeth," the young doctor said.

The wife reached past the cracked lips, into her husband's mouth. She plucked out an incisor. One by one, she yanked his remaining teeth and formed a tidy pile on the carpet. Then she cradled his head and removed his hair, which felt like pulling weeds. With a few brushes of her fingertips, his eyebrows scattered like pollen.

The husband didn't struggle. His breathing was slow and deep. Inside him, the darkness was abruptly saturated with light. He could see. He floated on a river under a pale sky. He felt clean and untroubled, and when he tried to recall his life before this moment, he saw only blue, and he understood that the blue was him.

The young doctor had gone to his car, and now he returned with a surgical saw and black medical bag. "Does your daughter want to watch?"

"If she does, she wouldn't admit it."

The young doctor nodded. "But a word to the wise—she might never forgive you for doing this without her."

The wife gathered her husband's teeth. She unfolded the cloth napkin and mixed the teeth with the vase shards. Then she carried the bundle to the kitchen.

"Grab the cutting board while you're in there!" the doctor called.

The kitchen lights were off, but she could see by the moon. She tossed the napkin into the garbage below the sink. She brought a fresh bottle from the pantry, uncorked it, and poured a glass. From upstairs, the daughter's music resounded: *Sometimes when the cuckoo's crying, when the moon is halfway down / Sometimes when the night is dying, I take me out and I wander around.*

In the living room, the young doctor had rolled the husband onto his stomach. Couch cushions elevated his torso. Obeying the young doctor's gesture, the wife slid the cutting board under the husband's face.

The young doctor wriggled his fingers into latex gloves. "Force of habit," he admitted, somberly.

The wife's hands shook so badly she had to set her wine on the coffee table. She thought she was prepared, but her face felt numb. She tapped a cigarette out of the pack. She noticed that the young doctor was staring at her with his insistent, demanding eyes.

"I don't want to bilk your money. I love you. And I make more than you, anyway."

The wife wasn't sure she'd heard correctly.

The teenage daughter appeared in the entryway in her pajamas. Black eyeliner, dripping, had clowned her cheeks. Her hands held a stack of paper.

"Is that a report for school?" the wife asked.

The daughter scoffed. "It's a report for life, Mom." She stepped into the living room and regarded the husband face down and hogtied upon the couch cushions. "Kind of ironic," she smirked.

"No," the young doctor corrected. "It's a surgical procedure."

The daughter padded across the carpet, barefoot, aggressive. "It's ironic," she hissed. She tossed the papers at the young doctor's face, but he deflected them with a raised forearm.

"What was that music in your room?" the wife said.

"What are you doing to my daddy?"

"It's simple," said the young doctor.

"I didn't ask you!" the daughter shouted. "This is his book." She indicated the scattered sheets. "If you had bothered to read it, you would know that his father was beheaded in a POW camp. Or maybe you did read it. Maybe that's where you got the idea! I wouldn't put it past you."

"I assure you," the young doctor said, displaying no discernible emotion, "that this is a necessary precaution to save your father's life."

With these words, the daughter wilted. The young doctor embraced her, patting her back. She cried into his shoulder. "Please, do the honors," he whispered.

He reached into his bag. He put the saw into the daughter's hands and then found a seat near the wife's legs, one of which he stroked reassuringly.

The daughter, on hands and knees, crawled to the husband's head. She lowered the blade and seemed to watch from a great distance as the teeth bit into the papery skin. For a full minute, she sawed. At last, the head separated from the body. The young doctor said, "Well done," snipping the remaining veins with scissors.

Nothing changed. The husband's body reposed. Scant blood stained the cutting board. The young doctor presented the hairless head to the wife's lap. The single eye stared. The gummy mouth hung open.

The daughter sawed the ropes that bound the husband's wrists. Then she stood. She embraced the young doctor. She kissed his hair and said, "You smell nice."

The husband's headless body rolled onto its back. It sat upright and bear-hugged the young doctor's waist. The young doctor made a low noise of despair in his throat when he realized he couldn't break free.

The husband pinned him to the floor. The wife, whose tears fell on the husband's gray face, heard the young doctor grunt, "Please don't," when the teenage daughter came at him.

The wife saw her daughter crouch beside the young doctor, and she understood what was happening. Her chest vibrated with pride. Of course, she thought.

The wife was surprised that the young doctor continued to speak while the saw teeth cut into him. His panicked eyes found the wife. He said, "Stop this. Touch him." The blade sunk deeper. Blood rose and spilled. He said, weakly, "You love me," and then his words were gargles. His spinal cord severed with a dull pop. In death, his eyes defaulted to desperation.

Two headless men spooned in the blooming pool.

Panting, the daughter held the young doctor's head in her lap. "It's heavier than I thought," she remarked.

But the mother was not within earshot. She was running up the stairs, running with purpose to the bedroom in search of the sewing kit.

TARZAN IN SPACE

ANTHONY MALONE

I NEVER WANTED TO BE an astronaut—I get dizzy standing up. So when they came for me in the middle of the night, shook me awake and said it had been decided, there were no others, they were going to send me into space—I said forget it boys, I'm just not up for it. They smiled and said "Actually, Gordon, that's not the way it works around here..." and the next thing I knew I was dragged from my bed and rushed out into the night air, my protestations ignored. See, all that stuff about astronauts being willing participants, gung-ho fighter pilot types who couldn't wait to skip off the planet Earth, that all came later. In England in 1955 you were going up whether you liked it or not, and as I was lifted above their shoulders and those scoundrels started taking me to the rocket I cursed the day I had ever gone to High Down to work for the British Space Programme.

It's just a ghostly set of concrete pads and blast chutes now but back in '55 the estate of High Down on the Isle of Wight was a top secret rocket testing and firing base and—if my new work colleagues had anything to do with it—it was to be the launchpad of my career as an astronaut. "God, no!" I screamed. "Come on boys, a joke's a joke!" But no use. They carried me past the blast chutes, past the silos for the eight highly modified V-2 rockets we'd taken from the Mittelwerk factory at the Mittelbau-Dora concentration camp outside Nordhausen, so much stubbier than the Saturn or Gemini rockets to come but far cheaper and more efficient. Right then I would have gladly seen each of them explode into flames if it meant I didn't have to go up in one. I pitched and rolled and begged and pleaded but they had my arms and legs and soon the small crowd held me aloft at the base of the largest rocket, the R-03, ready and waiting for months, the one with the third stage capsule, big enough for a man and set for space.

Until then I still believed they'd either made a mistake or the whole thing was a joke but it was when they started discussing amongst themselves how they were going to get me up the ladder to the nose cone two things became very clear to me. First: I realised they were for real and I was almost certainly going to die; and second: a single, droll, female voice cut through their drunken chatter like a V-8 through concrete:

"Let him go."

Women have such a civilising effect on men. Apart from the ones that start all the wars, of course. There was a momentary standoff, a couple of smart comments from the boys, then I was dropped like a sack of potatoes and left floundering on the grass. It turned out my fellow Instrumentation Officers, drunk as lords and not one of them over 25, couldn't quite compete with Jane from Hut 8, smoking a cigarette with a couple of the radar girls.

You could tell the chaps were embarrassed, didn't quite know what to say as they slunk away, claiming they weren't really going to send me into space—which is fine in retrospect, isn't it?—trying to rope the girls into the fun by suggesting a party in the bunker. Some of it worked and pretty much all the other girls drifted away with the chaps leaving me on my hands and knees, and Jane, finishing her cigarette and looking at me coolly.

She took a long look up at the rocket, exhaling smoke at the silhouette against the night sky. "You shouldn't take any of that personally. That lot are going stir crazy. They'll do anything for a laugh. I'm Jane. You are?"

I told her I was an Instrumentation Officer and first aider and she asked whether I was replacing the chap who left, the one so disillusioned with the lack of actual rocket activity he went back to Cambridge. I was bemused and didn't know what to say. "I just want a quiet life," I mumbled.

"You might get that here. Get used to the pranks, though. They'll only stop if they actually find a pilot for one of these things."

I got to my feet. "Professor Bailiss said…"

"Bailiss is a desperate old fool. This thing will never go into space. They haven't got a pilot. Unless you want to volunteer. A few more weeks of this and the Treasury will shut us down, you mark my words. So if it's a quiet life you're after, stick around. You might get what you want."

I didn't know what to say. She was a bit of a frost and I was wary of pursuing so I just watched her saunter off as it started to drizzle. I was still so shaken I just pinballed around the place for a while, ended up tramping over the fields at the back of High Down estate, thinking bitterly about my so-called friends and their prank and Jane and the lack of a real astronaut stalling the project, possibly for good. Right then I wasn't sure if I'd ever felt so low or, at least, so damp, and as if in response I was overtaken on the tree-lined perimeter road by a set of headlights coming up behind me. Squinting into the beams it was only when it overtook I realised it was a great military truck which sent a huge wash of muddy water over me as it passed. I shouted and spluttered and nearly broke my neck in a ditch but it didn't stop, just thundered on regardless which was pretty much the cherry on top of the cake that evening. Or so I thought.

It was only five minutes walk back to the main camp along the road but I was sure I'd caught a cold along the way. When I got there I noticed the military truck parked outside the medical hut and something made me stop behind the storeroom wall and peer back round even though the weather was dire. There was a sudden, silent, hairline fracture in the roof of the world and in the flash of light I saw the back of the truck had been rolled up and four squaddies had jumped out and were untying tarps and pulling down a ramp. There was a distant rumble, but it wasn't thunder; it was a vast tea chest, roughly ten feet by ten, and with great care the squaddies guided it out of the back of the truck, down the ramp and onto the gravel. The four men slid metal pipes through hoops on the sides of the crate and then, huffing and puffing, they lifted that great box off the ground and started taking pigeon steps towards the wooden hut. They got half way up the steps when one of them missed his footing, released the crate and pitched the whole thing onto its side. The result was a furious, primal bellow from within the crate itself.

The noise was such a shock it made me flinch back behind the wall and when I peered out again I saw the crate was rocking from side to side as if something within was struggling to escape. I would have said some*one* but none of the shouts and cries I could hear made any sense to me: *"Majambazi! Mashetani! Huru mimi, ebu mbwas!"* all of which sounded like Bailiss off his head on brandy. There was another fork of lightning and the rain started driving more insistently but despite the shuddering the young lads managed to lug the crate up the steps and once at the top they pushed and slid it the remaining distance into a storage room inside. Through the single latticed window I could just make them out standing around rubbing their chins until one produced a hammer and started pulling out the nails. That turned out to be a very bad idea indeed.

There was a lull, then a bellowing roar. Silhouetted in the window I saw a blur of motion, a dark shape moving fast, arms flailing and then, as God is my witness, one of the soldiers smashed through the wooden side of the medical hut, propelled by some unholy force and landing on the ground amid splinters of wood. There was a series of shouts and roars from the hut and then a melee of activity as the soldiers used the butts of their rifles to subdue their opponent. I cowered behind the wall, scared witless and wondering what the hell I'd walked into at High Down. Clearly, they'd hired one of those satanic army fitness instructors to lick all us chaps into shape while the space programme was stalled and he sounded like a monstrous rogue. I lingered while the hubbub quelled, then turned and scurried through the shadows back to my room.

Anyone ragged, spurned by a beauty, scared witless and soaked half to death in one night would have skipped town after all that, yet I must admit my only motivations to get up the next morning were professional obligations and the chance of seeing a bit more of Jane at the Monday morning meeting. I dressed quickly and sloshed down a cup of Yorkshire tea and headed over to the main bunker, trying to make light of the previous evening's prank. I wondered (hoped, actually) if it was to be that morning Professor Bailiss conceded defeat and announced the closure of the project. Bailiss—Nobel Prize nominee, bridge champion and part-time gravedigger by the look of him—stood in front of the clutter of chairs and affected Olympic disdain. When silence fell, he began:

"Gentlemen, the *babushkas* at the Ministry of Aeronautics have the results from last week's test firings and I'm sorry to say they report no luck in finding an RAF pilot willing to join us.

Tolstoy himself would have difficulty believing it. However, it is high time we stopped sending canaries and goats and bloody farmyard animals into the great blue beyond. I'm sure you're all as sick of mucking out the capsule as I am. So: I am pleased to say that as of today the British Space Programme has found its first astronaut."

There was a gasp and then pandemonium, cheers and whoops and immediate questions but I was worried for a moment that he was talking about me. Bailiss waited for everyone to calm down and then continued. "Our man—we're to call him 'Pilot X'—comes to us courtesy of the Royal Geographical Society. He is English, obviously, but with a somewhat unorthodox history. He has been flown in from the jungles of Borneo where his time has mainly been spent, ah, eating healthily and doing an immense amount of physical exercise. He is therefore ideally placed to withstand the vagaries and vicissitudes of uncharted space. The Royal Geographical Society maintain he has an abnormally prolonged life span which is either an advert for the virtues of the kumquat or a damning indictment of the British establishment, take your pick. Either way gentlemen, our time has come:

"England is going into space."

THERE ARE A THOUSAND different things that can happen when you start a rocket engine and only one of them is good. In 1955, no one had any idea what would happen to a man in space. Some thought he would go mad. Some said zero gravity would make his internal organs fly apart. Others claimed he would fall victim to some disgusting space plague, while Bailiss himself maintained that if anyone did land on the moon they'd merely sink into a sea of dust. What I'm trying to say is the whole thing was a massive shot in the dark and despite our practice in static firings, sending a man up was another matter entirely. We were meant to always have one rocket ready to fly and at least two others undergoing tests, but the lack of a pilot and the slow attrition of our skills had made us sloppy, which meant some furious activity over the next two days. I spent the time fine-tuning my kit, getting ready to track apogee and perigee radii, angles of inclination, keeping an eye on velocity increments and raising an alert if the mean pointing error of any second and third stage launch exceeded 0.25 degrees, and every time Jane walked past my desk I forgot my name and where I lived. Around me were the rows of desks where the other Instrumentation Officers sat, in the next room Jane and the other radar girls ran through endless practice scenarios, on the launch site the rocket engineers and technicians swarmed over the R-01, even the RAF helicopter was ready at Gosport helipad to retrieve the capsule as quickly as the seas of the channel would allow. It was 1955. Not all of it was bad.

As our mechanical clock ticked down to the launch, we were all at our desks in the bunker waiting for confirmation from the squaddies that Pilot X was in the capsule ready to go. Bailiss played with his pipe impatiently and lent towards the microphone. "How's it going up there, boys? All set?"

The tannoy crackled. There were sounds of grunts and then, "Get in, yer big oaf!"

A ripple of laughter went around the room but I was thoughtful. Sounded like he was being ragged, I could tell from experience. "First night nerves," said Bailiss, leaning around as the green light showed. "He'll be fine. Besides, we've got him strapped down... I mean, safety checks are complete. Right. Look out, chaps. We're going to light a fire."

I don't know if you've ever helped launch a stolen Nazi war missile, but if so you'll know what an absolute racket it makes on take off. It sounded like someone had thrown a drum kit down a fire escape. As Bailiss pushed in the firing pin we heard three distant bangs as the clamps were released, the retractable leads pulled away from the rocket, the gantry retracted and then the thing fired, eight gamma rocket motors spewing out ignited hydrogen peroxide and kerosene. We had test fired the rockets so many times we had it down to a fine art, but this one was completely different—it actually going up, even if it was just for a systems test. Apart from the noise, the actual firing was anticlimatic, yet when the R-01 went up in a perfect straight line we cheered and joined Jane and her radar cronies jumping up and down on the roof of the bunker, trying to catch a glimpse of the rocket and its mysterious pilot.

Then came the awful lull as we waited for news of a landing, safe or otherwise, and I'll never forget the euphoria when we got confirmation. Literally, people standing on chairs and hugging each other. That was almost matched by the groan that went up when Bailiss said the quad was to be quarantined and off limits to observers but we clapped and cheered as the helicopter brought the scorched capsule, battered and lopsided, swinging from ropes, back to the barracks. I remember Jane elbowing me as we milled around in the bunker drinking champagne from plastic cups. "You must be good luck," she said and I suppose then I thought maybe life wasn't too bad. Suddenly I had someone who might be described as a friend and the British Space Programme had a pilot and there was nothing, on that warm, bright, sunny day to suggest anything might be wrong.

That night I was brushing my teeth and getting ready to step into my sloppies when there were three soft knocks at my door. I groaned. Wary of becoming Pilot Y, I put my foot behind the door and inched it open. To my surprise it was Jane, lit by a shaft of moonlight and breathing heavily. She put a finger to her lips, slipped into my room and sat down on the edge of my bed.

"I hope you don't think it's fresh of me, but the girls in Hut 8 are awfully worried about Pilot X. I do so hope he's going to be alright in that terrible machine. You mentioned the other night, when I saved you from those horrible people, you were a first aider. I wondered would you let me into the medical hut? Just to make sure he has all he needs? I'd be ever so grateful."

I was contemplative. Frankly, she could have asked me to go up in the rocket myself and I would have slipped Pilot X a Mickey Finn and jumped to it, but thank God that scrumptious manipulatrix wanted nothing so prosaic. I rose, stubbed my toe on the leg of the table, and between gritted teeth agreed to what she proposed. Moments later we were walking from quarters across the quad and into by far the maddest—and possibly not entirely legal—endeavour of my life.

It was a chilly night and we crossed the quad alone. We went up the same steps the squaddies had heaved the crate and I unlocked the rickety wooden door of the medical hut. We passed by the storage room and took a left at the end of the hall, entering a long bare room dotted with the frames of empty beds. At the far end was something quite out of the ordinary. Against the wall, supposedly awaiting returning astronauts, was a huge decompression tank, built from metal struts painted yellow with a reinforced glass window bolted into the front. The place was silent. The shadows were deep. The squaddies nowhere to be seen. Jane and I walked up to the tank, pushed our noses close to the thick window and peered inside.

In the gloom, we could just make out a man on the floor, apparently asleep, naked but for an antelope-skin loincloth. The metal frame of a bed had been overturned and slung across it was one of the pressurised air suits the RAF use for high altitude flights. The man was a colossus, he made Charles Atlas look like Tom Thumb. I tapped on the window several times and eventually his head rose slowly and he looked at us for the first time.

He looked the way I often felt at a party—totally at a loss, uncomprehending, thoroughly miserable. He was also heavily bruised, swollen around the eyes and mouth and bleeding from several cuts. More to the point, I had never seen a man so out of his wits with fear; his tanned and chiselled features were etched with apprehension. I threw a glance at Jane and was struck by how affected she was. She was flushed red, breathing heavily, and biting her bottom lip. "Are you alright?" she mouthed through the inch-thick glass at the weak and dehydrated figure on the floor. She tried the door as well, rattling the handle furiously, but it was locked, so she beat her fists against the window to no avail.

"Willing volunteer, my eye!" she hissed, struggling to hold back the tears. "This is not going to stand." I looked backwards and forwards between her and the figure in the tank, terrified Jane was about to drag Bailiss from his bed and get him to release a violently deranged jungle Goliath onto camp. Thank God distant sounds disturbed us and reluctantly we withdrew, but we were both dumbstruck at what we had found. It hadn't exactly been the sort of romantic night I would have planned, but I consoled myself that ending the evening morally conflicted and worried about the future was par for the course when it came to dating. We separated and my love—I mean, Jane from Hut 8—disappeared, brooding darkly.

I spent a restless night plagued by dreams of Pilot X trying to spear me from a circling rocket and the next morning as staff gathered once again to discuss preparations for the second flight I only managed a place at the back of the room just as Bailiss, like a lamb to the slaughter, asked if there were any questions about the planned test flight for the next rocket, the R-02. I watched as that gorgeous, valiant woman slowly raised her hand.

"Professor Bailiss, has consent been obtained for all this?" asked Jane, innocently.

"I'm sorry, my dear?"

"Is Pilot X a willing participant in this great endeavour? It could skew the data, you see."

The atmosphere in the room subtly changed. There was silence from the chaps but you could see Bailiss had already twigged she'd somehow visited the medical hut. He smiled at her kindly, like an executioner. "Our pilot has wrestled crocodiles, Miss Porter. I doubt the airless vacuum of space is going to trouble him."

Jane persisted. "So he's not been beaten black and blue, then?"

This time the silence was excruciating. Then Bailiss played a blinder. "It's space that does that," he said. "Amazing, isn't it? Enormous forces involved, hence any bruising."

Jane swallowed hard. "He's not being coerced into this, then? Mistreated in any way?"

"Miss Porter, if our pilot was being mistreated I would be on it like a Romanov on a Fabergé egg. But he isn't, so I'm not."

"He'll be happy to give interviews then?"

Bailiss rolled his eyes. "That's a little optimistic, I'm afraid. Pilot X lacks your linguistic capabilities, Miss Porter. We will just have to rely on the electronic information. Which is what I'd like you to concentrate on collecting. Now, if there aren't any relevant questions I suggest we start the systems test on the R-02. We've waited long enough."

Stalemate and Jane might as well have tried to teach Urdu to a badger for all the good it did because we seemed to race through the preparations for the next flight. So to mutinous staff and a reluctant pilot were now added inadequate preparations which fed into the sense that sooner or later something was going to go horribly wrong. Still, three days later the R-02 launched perfectly. It's purpose—and the extent of its fuel—was to send Pilot X to the very edge of space, not beyond, at which point the capsule would be fired and it would drift down rather pleasantly by parachute with, we hoped, our pilot intact. It all sounded entirely reasonable the way Bailiss explained it, except the capsule on the way down clipped the wing of a patrolling Armstrong Whitworth Sea Hawk, sending it tumbling into the ocean. Worse, it landed in the sea directly in the path of HMS Vanguard which sailed straight over it, the capsule forced under the freezing waters and bobbing back up again like a cork; it must have been like a washing machine inside. Could an ordinary test pilot have survived that? Possibly with training, but Pilot X had spent his days riding elephants and spearing fish so even Bailiss was worried about this one. The capsule was returned very late at night to High Down,

I know because Jane and I skulked in the fields all night waiting for it and eventually we watched as that tin can finally made landfall, the ropes dropped from the helicopter and two soldiers approached the door of the capsule, unbolted it and stepped in.

They must have unbuckled the straps. Maybe they tried to rouse him or gave him a shot of something. All I know is that Pilot X—or at least a lunatic resembling him—appeared in the door of the capsule looking like Dracula's stunt double, red-eyed and sheet white, frothy at the mouth, but above all a look of abject terror on his face. These days any bog standard GP would diagnose post-traumatic stress on sight but the past is a foreign country. The soldiers around the capsule immediately raised their rifles, a net and then canisters of streaming gas were fired at him and Pilot X clawed at his throat and tried to run. His legs buckled, his eyes rolled, and he collapsed on the ground in front of the battered capsule.

Yuri Gagarin and Alan Shepard both got tickertape parades. Thousands filled the streets.

What were we meant to do? Sit there and allow this to continue? In secret conferences at the dead of night Jane and I agreed this was a scandal. "If nothing else it's a terrible waste," Jane breathed, chewing the end of a pencil. "Surely those muscles, that chest, could be put to better use…" and I nodded sagely and suggested a role in Physical Education or, at a push, the construction industry, anything other than being strapped to the biggest rocket in history and fired beyond the wit of man. I noticed Jane paid more attention to me when I voiced such thoughts so I hammed up my indignation in the hope she'd approve. In retrospect, that was an incredibly stupid thing to do because if I hadn't I might have been able to back out of what followed without a massive loss of face. We were in my room, the night before the third launch, when she leaned towards me and lowered her voice.

"Gordon, can you keep a secret? I can't say much, but my sister Beryl is going to be waiting on the perimeter road before the launch. If we could somehow free Pilot X and bundle him into the back of Beryl's Mini he could stay with her at her B&B in Torquay. I could perhaps visit and show him some of my schematics while he decides what to do. If we pop up to the nose cone before the launch and tweak the manual controls we can kybosh the launch long enough for me to release Pilot X. You do know where the manual controls are, don't you? You're so good."

I listened to all this and told her what every other sane man would have said to her; that she was battier than Bruce Wayne and her stupid plan would either get us both arrested or killed. It's just that the words came out as, "What a good idea. Count me in." I know this is going to sound stupid but I couldn't stop thinking about that crazy ape man propelled against his will into the cosmic dimension and I thought of how lost I'd felt at, well, every party I'd ever been to, and how out of my depth I'd felt joining the base and how Bailiss had sneered when Jane had expressed concern. It was then, in the faint light from the silver moon, I put two and two together and felt a strange kinship towards that kidnapped primitive and I reckoned in another life we might have been jungle brothers swinging on vines, showering under waterfalls, sharing a joke over a coconut but then, with a sinking feeling, I remembered I came from Guildford and my conscience—along with Jane from Hut 8—would never give me a moment of peace if I didn't do something to halt this astronautical wickedness.

So I suppose, for the record, that was the moment I decided to sabotage Britain's first manned flight into space.

WE CERTAINLY PICKED THE right day for it, that's for sure. Word had finally reached the Ministry that success might finally be within reach of the British Space Programme and the next day a whole host of top brass crammed into the bunker control room with us to watch England's first orbital spaceflight. "Is the monkey in the can?" Bailiss called over his shoulder to no one in particular, and then on the green light clapped his hands and rubbed them together. "Excellent. If this works," he murmured, "I'm going lather myself in ice-cool Russian émigrés." He turned round and caught one of the radar operators doing a monkey impression behind his back; armpit scratching, "ooh ooh, ee ee, ah ah", the full works. "Oh for God's sake cut it out! You belong in the Lubyanka!" he snapped, and then, spotting a frowning Admiral, he smoothed for Britain and turned away.

You could have danced a rumba round the room at that point and no one would have noticed so I caught Jane's eye and together we slipped from the room. We walked then broke into a run down the corridor to the double doors and out into the fresh air, the sound of the siren blaring across the grounds warning staff to keep clear of the impending launch. The sense of shared complicity in our illicit endeavour was intoxicating and as we legged it across the deserted quad I saw Jane's eyes flashing and her mouth was set. Plumes of vapour were streaming from the rocket then, that red and white chequered war missile brilliant against the clear blue sky, and faced with such an extraordinary sight I skidded in a puddle and almost did the splits. We reached the creaking step ladder at the bottom of the launch tower and started up the steps two at a time and it was then, suddenly fearful of the mad height and the thought of falling, I had second thoughts about what we were doing and for two pins would have left Jungle Boy to his fate except I'd gone up the ladder first and could not have descended with Boadicea beneath me. I fell out on all fours on the gantry bridge at the top, dry-heaving and sweating, and only pulling myself together when Jane stepped over me and the sight of those lovely legs heading over the latticed floor of the bridge brought me to my senses.

You don't really want to mess about with the nose cone of a rocket during the final stages of its launch countdown, and if we'd had a camera pointed at us then no doubt we'd be on YouTube these days, or in prison. Jane and I fell against the window of the nose cone and peered within. Pilot X was strapped inside, cocooned amid cutting-edge 50's space technology: ticking clocks, vacuum tubes, cables, plugs and sockets. His head was lolling, his eyes bulging, but when he spotted us—and by "us" I mean Jane—it seemed to give him a second wind and he started struggling against the belts. While Jane frantically motioned to him to pull off the sticky electrodes and help her at the window, I ran my fingers over the metal grips and smooth surface of the nose cone, searching for a small disc the size of a shilling and when I found it I pressed hard, causing a tiny door to ping open revealing manual controls for roll, pitch and yaw. That, unfortunately, was the extent of my knowledge—there's never a rocket scientist around when you need one, is there?—so in desperation I twisted them all randomly, praying it would do enough to confuse the circuits or stop the countdown or teleport me two hundred miles away. Jane had managed to pry the latticed window very slightly open, breaking the internal lock on it but I snatched a glance at my watch—we had less than sixty seconds to go—and yelled at her get to safety. With great bangs, cables started snapping from the side of the rocket and the gantry started to shudder, Jane screaming "Get out! Get out!" We both staggered back along the gantry bridge and slipped and slid back down the ladder, almost ending up on top of each other on the ground and as the sound of eighteen tonnes of kerosene and peroxide igniting filled the air we dashed back to the bunker, hands over our ears as the R-03 with Pilot X still inside powered into the sky.

    No one paid us any attention when we slipped back into the bunker, all eyes were on the black and white television set showing the image of the R-03 climbing ever higher. Jane and I couldn't look at each other. We had failed. Personally I would have liked to have been anywhere other than that bunker right then and I turned away, shut my eyes and wished, not for the first time, I'd become an accountant rather than an engineer.

Then—I remember this like it was a dream—someone near the television set said "Oh my God. He's climbing out..."

It was the damnedest thing. I turned back to the screen and saw what looked like an arm flailing from the window of the rocket, and then a head, and then shoulders. I have no idea how strong that wind must have been or what kind of strength you would need to cling on to the exterior of that missile, but cling that titan did, pulling himself out through the window and onto the red exterior, using the metal grips to hang onto the side and then pulling himself upwards, painfully slowly, but eventually falling down flat on the very nose of that ascending rocket. We watched in horror as the figure fought to push himself onto all fours and then managed to get into a squat on the top, one hand holding the top most grip. Then, as wisps of cloud began to shoot past, every stuffed shirt and boffin in that room saw Pilot X beat his chest and throw his head back and over the crackling intercom we heard, almost muffled by the roar of the rocket, an extraordinary ululating yell, the call of the jungle I suppose, and I swear to God I was ashamed of my countrymen then for violently wrenching that extraordinary man from his natural context and sending him, via my well-meaning tinkering, to an almost certain death.

The rocket tilted and everyone gasped as the figure missed one of the grips and almost slipped but then he edged back towards the window, disappearing through the tiny gap to relative safety. You could sense everybody in the room wanted the whole thing over with then, that this was already a major embarrassment to the top brass, so our attention wasn't on the dials and read-outs when they lit into life, when the tickertape started chattering and the oscilloscopes started dancing. It was an eternity before I realised Pilot X, God bless him, had completely misinterpreted Jane's mimed instructions and stuck the electrodes back on himself and actual useful data about manned spaceflight was now streaming back to us, the first proof a man could tolerate space travel. Bailiss kissed the tickertape when he realised what was happening, did a little dance as the data streamed in, then stopped dead as it became clear the R-03 was tilting off course, that its ballistic trajectory had flattened out and only God or the rascal who had messed with the pitch and yaw knew where it was going to end up. Before long, binoculars were no good, then it had disappeared from the television set and Jane sat back from the radar and watched the tiny pulsing light indicating the R-03 had dwindled for good and with it went all our careers.

So much for a Union Jack on the moon. These days people get antsy if you make drastic business decisions based on incomplete, subjective data but back then we were still living on Spam. I was probably suffering from some sort of colossal vitamin deficiency. That, or love. I've certainly sent a few rockets to their doom on that account.

England never went into space, not on its own, and the huts and bunkers of the High Down site were stripped bare, the blast chutes closed, the staff reassigned. I know because I was there when the man from the Ministry came and locked the gates, and didn't I feel guilty as sin? Professor Bailiss was never seen again and when the powers that be requisitioned all data from the project they found the data gleaned from Pilot X had disappeared with him. You'll note the Russians went from Laika straight to putting a man into orbit so you can draw your own conclusions as to where Comrade Bailiss ended up. Siberia, hopefully.

As for me, I ended up in Dungeness recalibrating imported Polaris missiles and lost touch with Jane from Hut 8—what do you think this is, a fairytale? She married an army fitness instructor apparently, which I found as difficult to believe as the news of that customised Nazi war rocket found almost intact on the coast of Africa, the one with the Union Jack on the side, a story everyone said was a hoax but which lifted an enormous weight from my shoulders and gave me strength in the years to come. You see, before Gagarin there was Greystoke and on the odd occasions I do venture out of my comfort zone, my thoughts inevitably turn to that tiny figure on the nose of the rocket, forced to do something so completely unlike him and yet doing it brilliantly and I thank my lucky stars I'm only tongue-tied or feeling a bit lost at a party and not sitting on top of eighteen tonnes of liquid propellant. In the years that followed I never dreamed I'd see anything like what I saw at High Down, and yet Alan followed Yuri, Saturn followed Soyuz, and then one incredible day a heavily booted human foot touched the surface of the moon. It's just that even now, in the twenty-first century, if you asked me for one example of bravery in the face of the unknown, for someone going above and beyond the call of duty, someone feeling the fear and doing it anyway, if you asked me for one single name from all the great heroes of the human race, the choice of this mad old man would be but a twinkle in my eye, a finger to my lips, and a letter, not a name, that once and forever made us all look up.

BULL
★★ INTERVIEW ★★

CURTIS DAWKINS

Curtis Dawkins often talks about how reading and writing saved his life. Given how that life will be spent behind bars in Michigan, I can believe it. Curt is by no means an innocent man. But you can see a searching life inside his writing, and a reason to live despite it all.

I visited Curt the week before I moved from the Midwest. The one thing I remember most about his prison is the sheer force that permeates everything. No door ever shuts; it slams. Even the vending machines in the visiting room seemed loaded and ready to snap back on my hand. We sat on plastic chairs and drank Cokes and ate pork rinds and talked.

This interview began during that meeting, and ended by talking to Curt on the phone, fighting through an awful connection fraught with echo and delay and ultimately a limited amount of time he could spare before returning to his life at the Michigan Reformatory.

—Jarrett Haley

JH: Usually location isn't too terribly important to an interview, but in this case, and in regards to your work, it's everything. Can you let us know a bit about where you are and how you got there?

CD: Of course, yeah. Prison colors everything, for everyone involved. But I want to say this first, as a sort of caveat: Whenever I speak about what happened to get me sent to prison, I'm always afraid that the ten years since that night will come across as sounding uncaring, unsympathetic about the man I killed, his family, my partner Kim and my three kids, my family—everyone traumatized by that night. It's still painful, but I've had many years to talk about it, almost clinically, as facts. It was a horrible ordeal and I still struggle with guilt and sorrow. There's often so much sadness and grief in my heart it feels like it might explode. But you learn within 24 hours of hearing that door slam shut, either you will die regretting the past, or you'll learn to live in the present.

So presently I'm at the Michigan Reformatory (MR), which is one of three or four prisons in the Ionia, Michigan area. I'm in a little, stuffy two-phone room on the 4th floor in the Level 2 side of I-Block, which doesn't mean a thing to those who don't have a loved one in prison, but level 2 is supposed to be a step up from level 4—and it is to a certain degree, depending on where you're locked up. I've been at MR for 3 ½ years, before that I was at Brooks Correctional in Muskegon. I am about 10 years into a life without the possibility of parole sentence for a felony murder jury conviction. That's how I got to where I am, but how I got to do this interview is a much longer story that begins with a poem.

JH: What poem?

CD: "The Love Song of J. Alfred Prufrock"—T.S. Eliot. I read it when I was a student, and it stuck with me after two years of community college, when I was just sort of floating around. After the family meat packing company burned down, I decided that I might like to try writing because of that feeling of kinship I felt with Prufrock; I identified with how he felt weird in social situations. And the one line: "till human voices wake us and we drown." I mean, that's amazing. That sounds as fresh today as it did nearly 100 years ago. I wanted to do that. I wanted to try and make people feel like I felt in that class, experiencing that poem.

So I started writing stories and poems, and I won an Illinois Arts Council Award with a story I wrote as an undergraduate. That story eventually got me into the MFA programs at Iowa, Emerson, and Western Michigan. I went to Western because I admired the faculty.

JH: Do you remember the story?

CD: Oh, yeah. It was called "Mother," about a son and his single mother eating dinner near the pool at a Holiday Inn. On the trip home they come across an overturned car with a wedding dress covering the back window.

It was a pared down version of a 30-page mess I brought to workshop, and I wrote it after class that afternoon once I learned there was ten times too much stuff going on. So I guess that was the beginning of trouble for me—I thought all of the stories were going to come that easy. It got published in a small journal and it was the best thing and the worst thing, y'know? David Foster Wallace said that the worst thing that can happen to a writer is publication before the age of 40. He would know. I didn't have success nearly as close to his, and that damn near killed me.

JH: How did it almost kill you?

CD: Well the stories definitely never came that easy ever again. Neither did publication. Years passed before I ever had anything published. I guess it was depressing, but it's weird—the bad times never led me into any type of trouble. I was sober when I went to college the second time, up until I got some success under my belt and started drinking again—a recurring theme in my life from a pretty early age.

JH: What about success got you drinking again?

CD: It's a pretty standard truth in addiction that success is more dangerous to sobriety than failure. I think that's because the addict thinks, "Wow, things are going good. I can drink and use drugs now." That, and anytime I felt good I always thought, "I can feel even *better* if I drink this whiskey." And there's an element of wanting to celebrate good fortune. We're wired that way. Cavemen probably ate themselves sick in celebration after they killed a big goat or woolly mammoth or whatever.

JH: And from an early age?

CD: The first time I had unlimited access to alcohol, something just clicked. That idea of something "clicking" is pretty common among addicts. I suddenly felt like I belonged. The unlimited access was a keg of beer for all of the employees of our family's grocery store/meatpacking company after we won Best Summer Sausage in the nation at the American Association of Meat Processors' convention. I set up camp around the keg and snuck drinks all night, then was sick as hell the next day.

JH: I notice we keep coming back to meatpacking.

CD: It was a big part of my life for a long time, being the family business. Meatpacking is actually a very complex and rich subject—the smells of spices, hickory smoke and freshly ground meat—the art and science of making those products is pretty remarkable. But all these companies that make products from animals: Farmland, Smithfield, Tyson, etc., they all use meat casings, which I eventually started selling to mid-sized companies in Chicago and the East Coast. This was after I got an MFA and pretty much "retired" from writing. I was tired of reading and writing and rejection slips. So I got into sales—not exactly the antidote for rejection. I started reading and writing again only after I ended up in prison. I was really fortunate to have that love to fall back on. Reading and writing almost certainly saved my life. I had to get out of my head, otherwise I was going to kill myself.

JH: I would imagine that moment, when the door slams like you said, and you're there facing a future that seems unbearable—it must change how you think about life, what you can make of it, or how you can even endure it, that sheer amount of time.

CD: Prison is basically nothing but time. I mean, that's why they call it "doing time." This probably goes without saying, but when a person unaccustomed to being locked up gets locked up, survival, in the beginning, is all you can do. And this has nothing to do with the danger around you—it's your mind. I thank God I almost instinctively began thinking of a story to write. Within a few hours of going to quarantine—that's where you're sent after conviction and sentencing—I began thinking of the first line to a story: "Sicilian Joe was a saucier until a Cadillac hit him doing sixty and knocked the recipes out of his head." I had to write it down so it would go away. But after I wrote that down, other parts came up, and for that time, yeah, I wasn't thinking about my new life.

JH: Is that when the book started?

CD: Pretty much. Every story in the collection has some part that originated from something I heard or saw in jail or prison. Sicilian Joe was a man I knew in the Kalamazoo County Jail. I didn't write at all in jail though—that was the worst, even worse than it is here—but I remember a lot of it, and I surprisingly found a lot to work with.

But it happens all the time. I mean, even right now the following drama is taking place in the cells around mine: A kid went home today after six or seven years of incarceration. He promised his TV to a friend, but someone somewhere else promised the TV to a guy who put up some money. Now he wants his TV. Someone is greedy and is trying to pull the old "okey-doke." Somebody could end up hurt. Who knows what's going to happen? People get stabbed over much less than a used TV.

So I'll file that mini-drama away and it might come up someday when I'm writing something. It's real. It's the lives of the people in here, and I don't know—I guess I've always related more to people who have known this kind of trouble, who've up and done some stupid things, much more so than any famous athlete or movie star—someone held up as some paragon of success.

JH: Why is that, do you think?

CD: It's like leering at disaster. It's like watching Kennedy get shot even after seeing it probably a thousand times. The appeal of that is a mystery, but it's completely human nature. I was just always interested in people like prisoners, people who could live through an experience like this. I would much rather read about why Andy, down the hall in cell 32, who just told me this, married his wife 6 times—once in a Wal-Mart—for the fun of it. Why would a guy do that? It's absurd, but fascinating to me.

JH: I know instances like that figure heavily into your book, and it's often made me wonder about your process. Normally I could care less about a writer's method, but in your case I'm genuinely interested—obviously you don't have computers in there.

CD: Nope, no computers. We have email but not real-world email; it's a kiosk thing we get access to every so often. But I was lucky that when I first came to prison we could buy typewriters with memory—about 80 pages worth—which helps a lot for revision. But those typewriters can no longer be ordered for some ridiculous reason, which sure as hell makes it harder for the men doing legal work in here.

JH: What about physically—when and where do you get a moments peace? Are people over your shoulder, asking what you're doing? Do you take notes throughout the day?

CD: I get my moments of peace at night, mostly. After about 10 p.m. prisons are usually very quiet. My schedule now is much like it was in graduate school. I have a little book light that I use every night, generally going to sleep at about three in the morning.

During the day, when I'm typing whatever, guys often ask what I'm always writing, and I have learned to say, "Letters." It saves tons of time to just say that, and in a way, it's true.

JH: What about outside of writing, just your everyday life? I imagine the close proximity amplifies everything in there—principles, values, or the lack thereof. Everyone and everything condensed, every facet of life, that is.

CD: I've said this before: prison is an Ivy League of human interaction. It's an education you cannot get anywhere else on earth. If you can get along with these men, you can get along with anyone.

Most of the time they just don't know how to trust. They expect to be screwed and ripped-off and beat up. That's all they know, so with that as a background, niceness and respect are seen as shortcomings. In that sense, prison is a rough, mean place.

JH: How much have you learned in there? You must have a unique perspective on the nature of men. I know you see the worst of it, but does anything good ever come? Any virtue in there?

CD: It's easy to generalize and say the men here are representative of the uneducated, no-good, downright evil male. But of course it isn't that simple. Some of these guys are funny and very kind. Listen to any of them talk on the phone to their loved ones: they love their kids and family deeply, are capable of all manner of good and bad things. They are intelligent in ways that wouldn't show up on the SAT, and most grew up in conditions of poverty and abuse that are hard to fathom. Most of them are in here for too long, and when they get out all they've learned is how to live in a cage. But we're all the same, people, I mean. It's good to realize that. Inmates are people, not villians. If there's one thing I hope my book will do, it's make it known that what is seen of inmates in the media, and what's portrayed in movies and TV, it's only the surface—if not outright bullshit.

Hopefully they'll come across as real people, not just the same clichéd approximations of prisoners. That's my goal, at least—to tell the stories first of all, and second, open eyes to the fact that the 2+ million people behind bars are people, not monsters.

When someone realizes how easy it is to get here—and it is, really, a good percentage of inmates went out for a night of fun, things happened, and here they are—they can have a little more compassion for the ones who are here, because if it can happen to you, or someone you love, you can see the point of showing mercy. Otherwise you can't.

But first come the stories. That's always first, though it took me a long time and many years to really realize that.

JH: "First come the stories"—what do you mean by that?

CD: I just don't think it makes for good art to start out with a lesson in mind. You can learn things from fiction, sure, but that's a by-product. Any discerning reader can spot those stories with a "purpose," like a fake Rolex. Just tell what happened, a teacher used to say to me. That's hard enough. It's all I can do, anyway.

COUNTY

AN EXCERPT FROM:

CURTIS DAWKINS

SICILIAN JOE WAS A saucier until a Cadillac doing sixty hit him and knocked the recipes out of his head. There was a faint line like an old smooth weld across the length of his forehead and the pale dots of suture scars. He wasn't five minutes in our cell before he knocked on the scar with his knuckles, making a dull metallic sound like he'd flicked an open can of soda with his finger. "Go ahead, try it," he said, taking a step closer.

"I heard it. I believe you," I said from my mat on the floor. Joe looked around our cell for another taker, but Domino—a snowblower thief and constant sleeper—and Ricky Brown were both dozing.

Normally I'm not a good conversationalist, but the past two months in jail taught me I had nothing better to do. So if someone talked to me, I had resolved to take him up on it. At least until he got boring, or until the lies became too much, or until *The Price Is Right* came on. Since it was only 10 a.m. I said, "How long ago did it happen?"

"About fifteen years." Joe sat in quiet reflection on the bench of our metal picnic table. "And the funny thing is, I was only visiting Cadillac for the day. My sister had begged me to come up there and meet her newest husband."

The television hadn't been turned on yet and Joe looked up through the bars to the cold, black screen we shared with the neighboring cell. I looked forward to seeing Bob Barker up there, and hearing Rod Roddy calling people to come on down. For an hour a day I could live in a world full of lights and color, noise and smiling women gracefully highlighting things with the near-touch of their hands. And hope. The hope for a good outcome kept me transfixed daily.

"Hold on," I said. "You were hit by a Cadillac in Cadillac?"

"Ain't that some shit?" Joe said. He turned away from the television and I could see his other scars then, some self-made, like the ones cut vertically through his eyebrows and the tiny notches in the rim of his right ear. "I was crossing the street to get a pint of gin and a pack of squares, then BAM! Doing fifty in a twenty-five. Knocked me eighty feet and out of one of my sneakers."

"Now that's something I've never understood," I said. "I don't get how someone could be knocked out of their shoes. And your case is even more bizarre because you were only knocked out of *one* shoe."

"There were witnesses," Joe said. "That's how the cop figured out how fast the guy was going."

"What law of physics governs whether a person's shoe comes off?"

And what are the chances a person gets hit by a Cadillac in a town called Cadillac? I wondered. Did it mean that everything meant something? Even if that something is a lie? And who's in charge of the meaning? And what the fuck could all of this possibly mean?

Ricky Brown woke up. He had been playing possum. Faking sleep becomes an art form in jail, especially when someone new comes in, especially when he's asking you to knock on his skull.

"I'll tell you what it means," Ricky said from his bunk. He always had the uncanny ability to answer the questions that were floating around in my brain, as if we were both listening to the same party line but he had a better connection. "It means don't pay a lot of fucking money for tennis shoes. And it means life is a big, shiny machine made by General Motors, and it's a tale told by an idiot, signifying shit."

Ricky read a lot—Faulkner and Shakespeare mostly—so he thought he knew some things. He was a skinny, red-haired, old-school man with a tattoo of a court jester on his left arm and a green, faded wizard on his right. He had the giveaway constellation of a crack addict's scars up and down his arms, the exact shape a molten-hot glass pipe hidden up inside his sleeves. Even without seeing his shins, I knew there would be scars there too, the same pipe hidden in his socks.

"Yeah, yeah," Joe said. "Tale told by an idiot. Signifying shit. I like that..."

ADVANCE READING COPIES AVAILABLE

Email: editor@bullmensfiction.com

RIMER'S BOOTS

COLIN FLEMING

IN THE SUMMER OF 1968, I was content to be working on *The Nabob*, a converted tuna fishing vessel that docked at Oakland's Matson Wharf. It wasn't the most glamorous job, and maybe content isn't the right word, but I was okay with doing what was asked of me, getting paid for it, and following the ship's one rule: don't ask any questions. We'd load the hold with some not especially large quantity of goods—which often was driven out on the rickety planks of the wharf by a guy in a pickup truck that none of us would ever see again—and dispatch it in Seattle, Long Beach, or any of a number of ports up and down the West Coast. It was light-lifting, you might say, and if you worried that you were engaged in anything illegal, you could always rely on your ignorance to see you through, or pass any lie detector test.

Some guys—it was a crew of three or four, depending upon the time of year—got more nervous than others. Like Elston. He was from back East and used to fish out of Dennis in Cape Cod, going up to the Georges Banks. He'd lost a lot of crewmates over the years—four, anyway, which seemed like a lot to me—and you'd hear stories about how hardcore those East coast guys were. But after the cops came around a few times to talk to our skipper, Reggie Thorpe, Elston would start chattering to any crew mate in earshot that we were all done for.

"There's our last voyage. What the hell we been shipping anyway?"

Inevitably, someone would shout, between drags off a cigarette, that questions were strictly forbidden.

"Doesn't matter now, does it?" Elston would counter, sniffling a bit. The cop would eventually leave though, easy peasy, and Thorpe would order us to get ready for our next middle-of-the-night visit from a pickup truck. Soon the guys were calling Elston—whose nickname had been Ellie—Nellie, as in Nervous Nellie. Tough thing to live down on a ship of hard men, guys you didn't ask about their past. And if they were telling you about it, on their own, they were either careless, or telling you for a reason, to get some upper ground on you.

I had come from the East as well. Boston. After Korea, home didn't feel like home. My dad didn't like that, when I tried to tell him, but he knew how restless I was. We'd be on the back porch, and he'd be peeling an orange, in one piece, a skill I could never master. He was just so calm. And I'd be fidgeting, unsure of what to do next, if there could be anything next, or if the world, for me, anyway, was to be one succeeding patch of emptiness after another, a stark yellow lawn that led away from something—something almost too real—toward nothing. You just took that long road, and walked it.

My folks thought Uncle Hess's cottage up in Harwich, on the Cape, was just what I needed. Solitude, peace, quiet, all the pike and trout you could want in this pond not even 150 yards away. And time. To work on a novel, ostensibly, one which I knew I'd never write. That had been the plan, before the war. That's a lot of people's plan though. And when something is a lot of people's plan, it's not an especially real plan. It's something you tell yourself you're going to do, but it's that hunk of bait—and maybe there's no hook in it—that you keep out in front of yourself, never lowering your jaws, never wanting to have its taste in your mouth. You use it for conversation, with people you're trying to impress, and people you could care less about. And with yourself, a person who, depending upon the day, can fit into either category.

Time got awfully trippy in that cottage, which had a cranberry bog behind it, and the ocean about four football fields away on the other side, so that there was always a mix of fruit and brine in the air. Sometimes I felt like it was speeding up on me, given how one thought would superimpose itself over another in my mind. I'd look up at the clock and see that five minutes had passed, when it felt like I'd been brooding for five hours. My nerves were shot, and on the train back, as I looked out into the surrounding forest and saw a couple pheasants walking with their backs to the track, I noticed that I was trying to gauge the train's speed, and that I was trying to figure out that rate to decide whether or not it'd be sufficient to splatter me in a couple different directions if I chose to come tramping out of that forest and step in front of it.

I got home and told my dad that was it. I had to go. I had to walk that yellow lawn, and hope, maybe, that it would turn into something else, something more verdant, with a place for me along the way.

I cut all over the country, working one odd job after another. That can be such a literal term: odd job. I culled possums in a backwater Arkansas town where the creatures had the run of the place. I was a courier on a motorcycle in Tacoma, and joined a biker club, thinking these guys, anyway, were as restless as I was, and maybe I could write some great ode to that lifestyle, once I had lived enough of it. I dumped gasoline on forest floors in northern California as part of a controlled burn team. We'd gather in a stand 150 feet above the forest, a couple miles off, and drink beers and watch those flames have their way with nature, satiating themselves by doing, simply, what they were made to do, and I envied them.

Eventually, I came to Oakland and started working on *The Nabob*. I didn't fit in with the people you'd see during the day, in the city, and in San Fran. It was like this hippie fest. Music was pouring out of every building, every car. Walk three blocks and there was no way you wouldn't hear what bands like the Beatles, the Dead, the Jefferson Airplane and the Stones were up to. The music was exciting anyway, and a long way from what I'd grown up on in Boston—Shostakovich sonatas, Bach cantatas.

One night we were hanging out on the wharf, kicking around a soccer ball that a member of the crew—this guy with bright white hair named Cotton—had found. Of course, it kept splashing down into the water, and then we'd have to try and fish it out with a net. I figured the latest pickup truck was due in the next quarter of an hour or so, but it kept getting later, and later, and soon I was glancing towards the east, getting ready for the first rays of the sun. But this gray El Camino came gunning up instead. Ugly ass car, but stylish, sort of, in how boldly it stood out from that weather-beaten wharf. You could have taken a black and white snapshot of those rotting planks and told a tourist it was from 1897 and they'd believe you. Anyway, we'd normally handle the drop, and start loading the hold. You wouldn't see Captain Thorpe, but he came racing out of the ship this time. The guy getting out of the car nearly hit him with the door, that's how close he was. It was a short guy, but he looked like he should have been big. He had this lantern jaw, a real galoot's jaw. No facial hair, which a lot of people had back then. Black jeans, an unbuttoned flannel shirt, a homemade Doors T-shirt underneath. I'd say he was rawboned, except he was too small, like he'd been shrunk down from some classic old school longshoreman who'd spit in your eye then knock you on your ass. He leaned close to Thorpe, and spoke two or three sentences. Thorpe nodded, and paused for a second, apparently deliberating his next move. He shrugged, with his palms facing skyward, and tried to show he was angry by stamping his foot, but I've seen more convincing performances at community theaters. And then he called my name.

"Clark!"

"Yes, sir."

"Drag that hide of yours over here."

I flipped the still-wet soccer ball to Elston, and approached the El Camino.

"This here is Mr. Rimer."

"Just Rimer," he said, sticking his hand out. "You ready to go?"

I looked as questioningly as I could at Thorpe, who seemed like he wanted to tell me something, but was unable to do so in front of our new friend.

"This is a business associate of mine," said Thorpe. "He'll be making something for which I have already paid him. He needs a new assistant due to a, well, scheduling conflict. I thought you'd be the best choice. Given your background."

"What?"

"Elston said you were a musician. Back in Boston. Is that true?"

"No. I mean, I had a little formal training."

"That'll do," Rimer piped in, motioning me to the passenger side of the car. The inside smelled like antiseptic. "Don't fuck with my radio stations," he barked, as we left the wharf behind.

"Okay."

And then he let out a huge laugh.

"Fuck with them all you want, mate. It's cool. Cool?"

I TENDED TO THINK I was world-weary back then, a guy who had seen it all. I didn't faze easily, so when we drove into San Fran and turned off the main road by a dumpster at the opening of an alley on Telegraph Hill, with my companion informing me that we'd stash the car here—like this was a perfectly normal thing to do—I thought, well, here's another crazie, no biggie. You met a lot of weird people back then, self-styled characters who believed, in their heads, they were something they weren't. One old-timer would come down to the wharf every few weeks with a bundle of paintings on his back, cursing in Spanish and telling us he'd been kicked out of his homeland because Picasso had some grudge against him, given his superior skill. He was all right: a lot of seascapes that he said had all kinds of levels of meaning. The art critic Clement Greenberg was writing about him for some fancy New York City magazine, he liked to say. Fine, whatever, buena suerte, mi hombre.

"Are your ears ready?" Rimer asked, as we walked up the hill.

"Sure. What the hell. Real ready. Are yours? Your eyes ready? Your nose maybe?"

"You don't know who I am, do you?"

What do you say in that situation? Should I? You're probably a junkie. Maybe you're a cheap hood. Maybe you're a nutter. We knew this hippie who would go up and down the beach every day, smiling beatifically when he found an abalone shell, which he'd throw into this burlap sack he toted around. As gentle as can be. Liked to tell you to love people as you'd like to be loved. Quoted the Beatles a lot. And then we learned that he went nuts on peyote and sodomized a retarded girl outside one of the local schools, and a dog too, but that part might have just been urban legend.

We got halfway up the hill. Rimer was breathing hard. He wasn't an outdoorsman, that was plain. But then he raced ahead, and took a turn down another alley. Wasn't a trace of him by the time I got there, but there was a door. A small door—the top of it was at the height of my shoulder, and despite the Alice in Wonderland vibe, I figured what the hell, a job's a job, even if you don't know what it is exactly as you're doing it. It was dark inside, and tight—the walls seemed to be up against my shoulders. The door closed behind me and a light went on the second the latch clicked into place. There were posters from floor to ceiling. Rock posters in loud, over-bright day-glo colors. The names of the bands, in psychedelic relief, looked wet, like they were going to drip onto the floor. The Byrds at Avalon; Quicksilver Messenger Service at the Fillmore; Moby Grape at Winterland. I heard a sound like an intercom going on, and a voice spoke to me from the ceiling.

"Well? You coming? Just keep going down. It's two more floors. Better get moving before Viachaslav does. He'll be pretty drunk by now. I didn't get him his stuff yet either. And he can be weird with his gun, if he doesn't know you. Don't sweat the accent. He's more American than anything."

So he was a nutter, clearly. Maybe there'd be more pay because of it.

I found some stairs at the end of the hall, and went down a couple levels. I had no clue what to expect. Something outlandish or lurid, probably. Marijuana plants, under lamps, in all directions. Naked women, even if that was pretty humdrum at the time. But what I found instead was a room decked out in stereo equipment, with speakers where you never saw speakers. Some were mounted into the wall, sideways, at waist level; others hung from the ceiling, like sound-producing stalactites. There were a few records arranged in an accordion display on the floor, where Rimer hovered over them. I recognized some of the covers; Elston was a big fan of the Stones' Their Satanic Majesties Request—although it was way too overblown for my tastes—and there were Mick and the boys, along with that first record from Creedence Clearwater Revival, local guys who were starting to get played on the radio, in the middle of the night. We listened to their version of "Suzie Q" a lot when we were loading up *The Nabob*. But it wasn't the odd deployment of speakers, and the seven different kinds of record players I counted that blew my mind. It was the dozens and dozens of austere, beige-colored, graphic-free albums that covered everything that wasn't a speaker or record player.

"Look, guy… I don't know what I'm here to pick up, but why don't you just tell me, and I'll start lugging it out."

Rimer seemed disappointed, the way an old friend gets when you've not shown enough faith in him.

"We're just here to listen, for now. We'll get started later tonight. You don't have any priors, right?"

He smiled like it was comedy routine time, but he looked sort of serious too.

"What?"

"You haven't been pinched, in jail, charged, that kind of thing."

This was cryptic.

"No. No priors."

"Do you have any prior experience as an artist? That's a stupid question though, isn't it? An artist is never in the past. Not a true artist. There is no prior, there's just now, and next." He selected an album I didn't recognize from his batch on the floor, and placed the record on one of the turntables. "This is Blue Cheer."

"Like the kind of LSD?"

"No. Like the heavy rock band. Big lumbering sound. Loud. Sort of ugly."

I thought my ears were going to bleed it was so loud in there. Rimer walked around the room though, checking his mounted speakers, sometimes conducting the music with a pencil he waved through the air. The guy was utterly placid. When the record was finished, he motioned back toward the door, and asked me if I wouldn't mind waiting for him for a couple hours in this bar across the street.

"You'll be paid, of course, for your time. Our gig isn't until tonight. Probably. You drink?"

"Some."

"I have a meeting. With Janis. Are you a fan?"

I was pretty sure, by this point, he was one of those dealers who dips into his own stuff. But he talked with such suavity, this total assurance, like we were having the most regular of days together, and I began to wonder if dear old Captain Thorpe was having one over on me, largely humorless guy though he was. But he probably thought I was too.

"Because if you are a fan, I could ask her to sign something."

He reached down on the floor for another album. It was Big Brother and the Holding Company's Cheap Thrills. I liked that one a lot, actually. It was loud—not Blue Cheer loud, but plenty loud still—and the guitars were out of a tune a lot, but that didn't seem to matter. It was one of those records that was everywhere that summer, with Janis Joplin doing those vocals of hers that sounded like she was turning her entire body inside out. My parents would have hated it; they'd have said, come now, son, wouldn't you prefer some Brahms, but that music, to me, was the sound of what it felt like in that cottage back in Harwich, with the its smell of fruit and brine in the air, when I knew I had to leave, the sound of knowing you need to light out. From whatever is holding you back. Even when it's yourself.

"That Janis?"

"Yeah, that Janis."

"You work for her?"

"I'm trying to do something for her. I'm not sure I'm going to be able to though. It's a fine balance when someone doesn't want you doing for them that they need. But it takes all kinds of art and artists in the world, right?"

"So you're an artist?" I asked.

"Yeah. Well, it depends upon how you feel about the law, I guess."

THE BAR ACROSS THE street was as divey a place as I'd ever been in. There was a neon sign in the one window that flashed the word Remo's, with the "m" failing to light up. The decor was what you might think of as dirty nautical, like Captain Nemo had some wastrel of a brother who went to seed and opened a shit bar. Fishing nets with flakes of scales in them hung on each wall, with bait buckets—maybe they doubled as spittoons—in all the corners. There were some stuffed fish scattered around, but all of them seemed to have had a part snapped off—a dorsal fin, an eye, a bit of tail. The swordfish behind the bar had been relieved of his defining characteristic. The jukebox was draped in fishing nets too, so I was surprised when the one guy in the bar, besides the bartender, hopped off his stool and dropped a few nickels in the machine.

"Really, Slava? Again? You said you were going to try and give it up."

"I am, how you say, in between. I want to like, but I no want to like. Sometimes one more than other. I know I should not like. But then I think, 'Viacheslav, who are you, of all people, to say what is art, what is not art? Did you not once listen to recordings banned at home? Think how beautiful they were. Did you wish you could not hear them? No. Of course you wish.'"

He teetered as he climbed back on his stool, and downed the glass of vodka that was waiting for him.

"You—why you come? Young man. There are better places in the middle of the day for a young man."

"I'm working for someone. I think. He told me to wait here."

Slava and the bartender exchanged a look, and the former nodded, before pouring another glass of vodka.

"You wait for Rimer. He maybe tell you I have gun. Trying to be funny. Always changing everything. What is up is down, what is wrong, he think right. You must like music. We listen."

Who knew that some crinkly, drunken Russian would be a Blue Cheer fan, but there were those massive chords from "Summertime Blues," the song I'd been listening to a half hour ago. Or so I thought at first. They were clearer now though, even though this performance was from a concert, and those chords had a shimmering depth to them that made me think of waves of light. There was just the shabby jukebox speakers, but it felt like that music was on all sides of me, physical and organic, as though you could touch it, and could not avoid being touched by it. I'm not someone to put down someone else for doing what they do, if it's what they believe in, and I guess Blue Cheer believed in being loud as all get-out, but this was something way more, like you were in someone else's head, with all of the pride, and doubt, that went into that thing they made, that you were hearing. The concerns, the joys, the reservations. When the song stopped, it felt like I'd been dropped out of one world, into this waiting room in another, which happened to be this crap bar.

"So you have not heard Rimer's work before. Now you hear. No one understand how. Some say it is drugs, drugs in air. We all absorb drugs, Rimer put drugs in grooves of record. Some musicians want. Most, no. Too real. Rimer do not listen. Or he listen too well. Depends on how you think."

"You're saying he's a bootlegger? That's not so bad. I thought I was going to be running something hotter than that."

"Is not hot enough? I sleep now. For concert tonight. You tell him I still wait. He has money. Bad to make customers wait."

And with that, the beaten down old Russian tromped out of the bar, and the bartender passed the untouched glass of vodka down to me.

"Fucking thief, if you ask me. I wouldn't want someone making a recording of me talking to people while I'm working and playing it for everyone."

"Why do you have the records he makes in the jukebox then?"

"Why the fuck wouldn't I? People love them. They say he's a better artist than the people he records. It's fucking unnatural, but there it is."

I'D BEEN SITTING ON the curb outside Remo's for a half hour when Rimer finally turned up. He looked more flustered than I would have expected was possible with him.

"Bad meeting?"

"If you like tits it was good. She was a mess. Strung out on something, pulling her shirt up over her head. But she's pretty straight even then. Said there was no way she was going to let the label have me record her. Called it some voodoo shit."

"I heard as much."

"It's just my kind of art. Nothing freakier about it than that. You understand a space. I don't mean, oh, look, it's a room. But you understand how the backs of chairs, their shapes, alter sound, and how the curves of the roof alter sound, and you understand what a musician thinks about their sound, where they're coming from when they make it. You put it all together, and you know that if you're at such and such a gig, and the atmospheric conditions are a certain way that the bottom bass string does that, the snare drum does this, and you know where to stand, and how to turn, and you have the right gear, of course, you can get a recording that sounds more like that musician, that band, at the very core of who they. As people even. People like live shit, so they buy it. There's not a lot of it. That crap Stones album with all the teenyboppers screaming from a couple years ago. Who listens to that? But live is where it's at. Live is life. Sometimes people don't want it feeding back at them, no matter how well they're doing, or how hard people are clapping, if that makes any sense."

"And you sell it?"

"Of course I sell it. Anyone who's buying it is buying the official records anyway. It's not my fault that my stuff sounds better. The suits don't like that. A recording made by a guy with his gear strapped to him isn't supposed to be soundboard quality, you know, which is what you get when you plug into a console in the studio. Some people say my work goes beyond soundboard quality, but I'm no critic."

It sounded crazy to me. I understood that fans would want to buy more records by their favorite bands. They went to their concerts, after all, and here was a chance to freeze those memories and bring them back home with you, where they could be reheated again and again at the end of a stylus needle. But that there was someone out there who could view taping as an art form, with music that sounded different than you'd think that band was capable of making—well, I don't know.

"Anyway, we got to get you kitted up. Make sure you don't bang your hands against the clothes. The microphones are fragile, and they're all pointed the way they need to be pointed. We'll make a trial tape tonight. The Airplane is at the Fillmore. I thought they'd be canceling, since Grace Slick has been sick, but Janis said she's off what she was on, so we should be all right."

"I should probably phone the ship. I figured we'd have wrapped up our… business… by now."

"I already did. Thorpe's been waiting on some stuff. And since my last guy started running his mouth—and get shot in the head for it—there's been no new stuff. He said you're as tightlipped as they come."

I didn't know about that.

"Shot in the head? That's an expression, right?"

"Sure, if you want."

I HADN'T EXPECTED THAT EVENING'S Jefferson Airplane show to be the first of many that I went to with Rimer. It was a good gig, so far as my limited experience in these matters went. My job was simple, really: I was supposed to stand in the middle of the room, in a spot Rimer marked for me with some chalk on the floor, before the bulk of the crowd streamed in.

"You're not the music man. Don't sweat that. You're the depth guy. The crowd, the ambient sounds. It's a whole separate tape. Just do your best not to move."

And so I did. The Airplane was one of the bigger SF acts at the time. Maybe the biggest. Them or the Doors, anyway. They did their hits—songs like "White Rabbit " and "Somebody to Love" —but it was the more obscure stuff—like this extended cover of "Tobacco Road" that the crowd—the true cognescenti, I guess—went nuts for. The bass shook the floor, and I wasn't sure how the band were able to hear themselves up there onstage in that cacophony. But for me, everything—the band, the stoners, the occasional woman who flashed her chest, the couples groping each other against the walls—was secondary to watching Rimer. The guy was everywhere, crouching down, hopping in the air, turning his back to the stage on a given rhythmic accent, and then forward again on the offbeat. He seemed to anticipate every ebb and flow of sound, like he was choreographing it by the way he moved. For the opening verse of one song, he'd be in the back of the room; by the time Grace Slick laid into the first syllable of the chorus, he was in front of the stack of speakers on the right hand side of the stage. Sweat poured over him after.

"I think it was pretty good," he said to me when we were back outside, making a bee-line for his car. "Lot of planning, Clarkie, lot of planning. You need to try and be the sound, if you want to get the sound. Dig?"

We ditched the car in the alley with the dumpster; when we got to the door, Rimer looked around a couple times, like he expected someone to leap out of the shadows. The second we were inside, he practically ripped my flannel off me, and pulled out a spool of tape. He had several on his own person, and, just like that, there was a stack of black rolls in his hands.

"Alchemy time. We'll see what we got. Should be good enough to fill a bunch of back orders. Give me a few hours. I'll meet you at Remo's. If Viacheslav is there, tell him he'll have his stuff soon. If he's drinking."

I was about to ask what difference it made if he was sauced or not, but Rimer was gone, and the door to that audio chamber of his had been shut in my face. I sat down on the floor to gather myself. Thorpe had had all of us do some strange things over the years. I was only two months into my second year with him, and I'd already had a stint at a funeral home loading coffins into a Packard at three in the morning, and driving down to the wharf. Elston said some that some surfers had written it into their wills that they wanted to be buried at sea, which was normal enough, I guess, if you thought about it, but illegal all the same. But how many surfers die at once? Exactly. But like I said, you didn't ask, or you were out on your ass.

Whatever was going on here was less lurid, anyway. I was pretty sure of that. A beer sounded good after everything, and maybe the funny Russian guy would be there spouting off. I thought he was kind of Zen, almost. But what certainly was not Zen in the least was what I heard coming from the other side of that door. That rush of sounds nearly put me back on the floor. I thought I heard the voices of four or five men. There were a few seconds of music, at an overwhelming volume. Then something would hit the ground, and something else would thud against the wall. For all I know, someone had been waiting in there, and Rimer was getting the shit beat out of him. Maybe he was already dead. I tried the knob, but it was locked. There were a couple seconds of silence, and a voice answered me back. It was Rimer's.

"We're just getting started here. Tell Slava we got a good one, if he's drunk enough…"

Slava was indeed drunk. The place was packed, which shocked me. I figured it was the kind of bar that no one went to but the people in the adjoining buildings who had nothing else going on in their lives. A sad sack bar.

"I tell you: show tonight, dynamite. I think Janis Joplin best singer. Best singer of blues by women. In Soviet Union, no blues. No women blues. Songs supposed to be happier, but happy song that is not really so is very sad. So blues anyway. But not honest. Joplin, honest. I play."

There was a pocket of long-haired guys around him, and a few biker-type women as well. They looked pretty hard, but a couple of them patted Viacheslav on the back as he made his way over to the jukebox. Within a few seconds, Joplin was singing "Summertime," and everyone who had been talking shut their mouths—like there was a tacit agreement to do so—and listened. I had heard the song 100 times, probably. I enjoyed it, but then again, the Gershwins wrote material that was pretty hard to butcher. The cut finished, and another began, and for this, everyone who had been standing sat down. It was the same song, but a live version, and I knew, straight away, that it was one of Rimer's productions. There was so much depth to that sound that I wondered if I wouldn't get the bends if I moved too much while it was playing. Viachaslav's eyes were closed, but I could see tears coming out of them, as they were coming out from a lot of other eyes, as well. They were coming out of mine, before I knew it, and I didn't see biker chicks and stoners and drunks around me, but rather the edge of that pond in Harwich, and the pine forest on the western side of it. I saw those two pheasants in the woods, I saw that train going over me, and my mangled eyes, one on each side of the track. I saw those fields of dried, yellow grass, the future I had set out upon. And I saw, for the first time, vague shades of green off in the distance, and those shades undulating in the air, in time, like they were dancing to music. The song reached its conclusion. There was silence for four or five seconds, and then Remo's went back to normal.

"You. Young man. You come back. Better at night, yes? Have vodka? You share vodka, so I stay longer. I slow down."

He had a bottle in front of him, and he dumped some of it into my beer.

"You should have your stuff soon. He says it's good."

"What you think?"

"I haven't heard it. I don't really get what he does, or how he does it. It's all new to me. Way new."

"Is it? Or is it old made new?"

He leaned in close. I could smell the vodka in his shirt collar.

"He tell probably. Last assistant—I do. Not for music. He also deal heroin. And like you know, job is job. I not always do good job, but that is because of Rimer, I think. I can't help myself almost. How you say...turn blind eye. Blind eyes. I look past. In past. Little joke. What am I supposed to say—no more music like this? Is wrong? I know is wrong. Legal wrong. Person have no right to record and distribute music without consent. All kinds of wrong. Anyway, I no shoot assistant. Partner did. But I would have."

"What's your job?"

"Rimer no tell? Curious man. I customs. There is black market. Goods. Rimer know I am watching. But he say, 'Slava, if man cannot learn how to hear himself, man only a record no one play. Not alive. You try to hear, Slava. Here is what I do,' he say, and give me evidence after evidence after evidence. But I begin to hear. Even though it hard to hear. So I keep trying."

"And building a case against the guy who's hooking you up with that music."

"Rimer no care about case. Art is case. Music is case. Hearing is case. Me, I one case. Not important kind. You your own case. But you know now. You not know before Rimer. He know. So he not care about my kind of case. Legal case, music case--very different."

THAT AIRPLANE TAPE PROVED to be a massive underground hit. Rimer had a guy who worked at Elektra Records, who'd press up copies for him for a cut. We'd drive around town and unload them in the back rooms of head shops. A few cartons went to *The Nabob*. I figured I wouldn't be on this particular job much longer, but Thorpe told me to hang on for another week, and then I'd be back on my regular beat, if I still wanted it.

I wasn't sure. I had this curious sensation of wanting to light out again, but for something more permanent, more in one place. It felt oxymoronic.

We were hearing that Rimer's latest bootleg was outselling some of the heavy hitters—stuff like Iron Butterfly's In-A-Gad-da-Da-Vida and Cream's Wheels of Fire. The latter would stop Rimer cold whenever we heard a snatch of it.

"Listen to Ginger Baker on those drums. That was recorded here, at the Fillmore. Nothing to transport you. Music isn't music if it doesn't take you somewhere inside yourself."

He'd talk cryptically like that, but I liked him. A lot. I wasn't someone who made many friends, but I was getting a big kick out of the gigs we went to. Not so much what I heard at them. Which was fine enough. But that alchemy—I was living for that, to hear what Rimer would come out of that room with. I never knew where that music would take me, what experience from my past it would reframe, you might say, so that I could see it better. With each passing day, the music on those bootleg records got older, but the more you listened to them, the more you felt like you were catching up with your future, the future you were meant to have, if that makes any sense.

We'd hang out on the wharf, sometimes, and drink beers with the guys, with one of those Rimer boots—that's what everyone called them—playing on *The Nabob*'s hi-fi. People would wander over from the nearby warehouses, and you could see what the music was doing to them, the first time they heard it, that it was taking them somewhere, too. I noticed that the more bootlegs we made—it was funny how I thought I had some crucial role, like I was more than crowd/ambient sound guy—the less Slava drank whenever I saw him at Remo's. If someone put a Rimer boot on the jukebox, he'd walk out to the street, and smoke his pipe until the music stopped.

I was outside one night, waiting for Rimer to finish whatever it was he was doing to a Doors recording. The Doors were his favorite band. He'd lecture me on how Jim Morrison "got it," by which he meant that he wasn't locked in one place, in his mind, anyway. "He's like a traveler, a searcher. But not like John Wayne in that cowboy movie. He goes where his mind goes." Rimer was no stranger to that kind of fuzzy hippie talk, but there was more resonance with what he said, if you considered it against a backdrop of the music he helped make. He was creditable, but damned if you knew how he did what he did. It seemed like it had something to do with where you were in your life, and where he knew you were. There were a lot of people in those bootlegs, at different points of their existence. Somehow he got all of them in there, like his records had an infinite number of grooves, and you got your very own. I offered my can of beer to Slava, but he passed with a nod of his head.

"You don't like to listen anymore?" I asked.

"It is hard. Sometimes, what I see, I don't like. It can be hard to know what person is if person wants to be something else. I prefer regular music now. Buy from normal store."

"Maybe you'll feel differently in the future. You never know."

"I know. You know something else for you. Just like Rimer know something else for him. And us both. He understand. I hope you do too."

Sometimes, when someone is upset, they want you to say something, or touch them, maybe, but I could tell that Viacheslav, in that moment, wanted to be left alone. Still, I felt guilty as I drove Rimer over to Berkeley's Community Theatre, like there was something I should have been able to say. An old guy, alone like that—presumably, anyway—having to look at what he might have been, and what he wanted to be, and seeing that nothing measured up. I was on my way there myself.

The Doors were headlining, with Quicksilver Messenger Service and the Airplane backing them up. We were, so far as I knew, there to listen only. We found our seats, and Rimer said he had to check something out, and to sit tight. I waited until the show was about to start. Still no Rimer. The sound techs were all done with their pre-gig tunings, and just when you sensed the light would be going down, they got much brighter, and music started playing, although there wasn't a band on the stage.

The way I figured it later, Rimer had bribed one of the tech's to play his latest bootleg, something we did at a Doors show at Winterland a few days before. I had yet to hear the results, but as I listened to that music in that hall, with who knows how many other people, I knew—and it didn't take any figuring—that I'd be leaving San Francisco before the sun came up again, with a whole lot of dry, yellow grass to put behind me. A boot from Rimer had a way of reintroducing you to yourself, and what you really should have been up to all along.

But I hadn't expected to see Viachseslav, especially a fast, nimble version of him. He came running out of the wings, where Rimer must have been standing, because they both tumbled out onto the left side of the stage. Jim Morrison looked on, and Rimer got off the ground, without any struggle, and put his hands behind his back, where Viacheslav cuffed them. The music kept going, and I saw that Viacheslav was starting to cry, while screaming, in broken English, to shut that shit off, adding, just as loud, that it wasn't really shit, but it was wrong all the same. I heard something about legal cases, and music cases, and how they were very different, but he had a job to do. The music stopped, and everyone looked around abruptly, like each and every person there had to know if anyone else had felt what they had felt.

I was back East within a week. Elston rode with me. He wanted to get back to the Georges Bank, or away from Matson Wharf anyway, and said that the business with the bodies decided it for him, but I put it down to whatever he heard in those bootlegs. I said maybe I'd go with him, and make like I was Melville, but I understood that the only place I was going was back to that cottage on the Cape, where the smell of fresh cranberry and sea salt infused the air. There would be nothing for me there,

I knew, but I'd hear the place differently, and I'd hear myself differently.

When I got back to Boston a month later, to tell my father that, yes, I would write that novel, even if it turned out to be terrible, he handed me a letter from California that he had already opened and read. My parents were always on the nosy side.

"Only light sentence. I do last job then quit. Trying to hear again only right way this time. Even if hard. Rimer make records of this band you call Zeppelin and Van Morrison who is very different from others. I hear him well I think. Maybe I Irishman and not know. Some day maybe. Thorpe stop dumping bodies in sea. I tell, and he listen."

THE NAZI METHOD

CHARLEY HENLEY

I FOUND MOTHER OUTSIDE IN the chaise lounge, watching a TV she'd strung through the window of the double-wide. Flopped next to her on the patio table sat a large-print book on astral projection and a couple of her favorite crystals. This big chunk of obsidian and a thick slab of quartz. She's getting up there, Mother. Complains about her veins, her arthritis. But she's got a sharp mind. Still crazy as ever for that off-brand religion. Stray prophets and ancient texts. Alien monuments on the surface of Mars. She was dressed in her usual stretch pants and flip-flops. Had her T-shirt from the Worm Grunting Festival up in Sopchoppy. She was rubbing the crystals and going through the receipts from The Royal Palms. That's our motel. Or rather her motel. Which I manage.

"Aren't those our criminals?" she said, pointing at the TV. The screen showed grainy footage from a surveillance camera of two boys waving automatic pistols around a bank in Pensacola. "Maybe you ought to call the police."

"They checked out days ago," I said. Actually, they left in the middle of the night, having absolutely trashed our number 10 unit, down at the end of the motel.

"There was a fire fight," she said. "Killed a guard at the bank."

I popped the top off the beer I was holding and scratched my belly through my open shirt. It was one of Dad's old shirts, covered with mai-tais and naked ladies.

Mother looked at her watch. She shot me this long, deadly stare over the beer.

"Amounts to the same thing," I said, "whether you get drunk alone, or you're the leader of nations. That's JP Sartre."

"You should have never gone to college if that's all you were going to learn," she said. "Look at Rodger."

"The Cock-Doctor?" I said. My brother, the go-getter of the family. Skipping grades and getting scholarships. Now he's a plastic surgeon down in Boca Raton where he specializes in cocks. Claims he can find you another two inches in there.

"Don't be ugly," said Mother. "And speaking of those criminals, have you cleaned out unit 10 yet?"

We've got daily rates at The Royal Palms, or you can pay by the week or month. That's what these guys had done. They seemed all right when I first checked them in, but after a few weeks, this huge pile of garbage sat out front of unit 10. The Astroturf smelled of piss. They'd broken our patio furniture, ripped up the fence, tossed our pink flamingos into the scrubby junipers next to the Church's Fried Chicken. Then a few days ago they vanished. I'd only been in there to plywood the window and stretch caution tape across the door. The unit was a total loss, all Sudafed boxes and spent cans of Dran-O. The whole property stunk of ammonia. "I don't think it's healthy in there," I said.

"Rodger says not to call the EPA," she said. "We'll never hear the end of it."

He was probably right about that, though I wasn't going to admit it. And, of course, that was another good reason not to get involved with the police.

I drained my beer and slouched off down the blacktop, flip-flops slapping against the soles of my feet. But I sure as hell wasn't going straight down to unit 10. A man my age who lives with his mother—it's trench warfare. It's every goddamned yard. I had to let her watch me screw around for a bit. So I walked over to the bean-shaped pool and pulled a few leaves from the water. Then I wandered out to Highway 98, where I stood beneath our sign, this royal palm tree, painted pink and circled with blinking marquee lights. I listened to them clicking as they made their revolutions. Through the trees I could see the sunlight shattering in the Gulf. I spent a few minutes picking trash out of a squat butterfly palm, then I leaned against one of our tall sabals. A warm breeze blew against my skin, and I popped the last button on my shirt.

I watched this girl from unit 3 step out to the curb for a cigarette. Mostly we get retirees at The Royal Palms. Widows. Old ladies in muumuus, with accents out of Baltimore and Queens. Their husbands worked hard all their lives only to drop dead at the age of 64. Alone, they wander the flat white beaches of the panhandle. Nothing but dog-eared paperbacks full of hot Latin love to pass around the pool. That wasn't the situation in unit 3.

She'd cut her hair down short, dyed it blonde, and lacquered it stiff as plastic. Freckles spattered her cheeks, like something flicked off a spoon. She was thin as a cable whip, stringy-looking, and seriously pissed off. Beneath her cut-offs, I could see her legs were a mishmash of thick tattoos. None of it tourist stuff, dolphins and fairies. This girl had etched skulls and coiled serpents. Mother must've checked her in, as I hadn't seen her before.

"Good afternoon," I said, walking along the units.

"What's so good about it?"

"I don't know," I said. "Maybe it's a piece of shit."

She paused, then offered me her hand. The word FUCK was written across her knuckles. "I'm Ellie," she said.

"Cecil Boggs."

And with a jerk she drew me close to her all of a sudden. Took a hold of me, like. I could feel her knobby breasts poking through her T-shirt. "You got any pills?" she said.

Now, I'm a forty-three year old man who lives with his mother in a double-wide trailer. So if there's one thing I understand it's the value of a negotiated settlement. "You're talking painkillers?" I said. My brother, the Cock-Doctor, had given his new wife a set of tits and a nose to mark the occasion of their recent nuptials, and they'd been up to see us for a couple of weeks so she could convalesce away from the prying eyes of the social set down in Boca Raton. Let the bruising fade and the stitches heal. Prescription bottles had been falling out of her pockets. It was after they left, that Mother had come across an ample stash of Oxycontin.

"How many you got?"

I looked back to where Mother sat watching the TV. She was rubbing the obsidian against the screen. It was Judge Judy on there, and I assumed she was trying to purge the evil out of one of the litigants. I turned back to her and said, "Why you got those numbers tattooed to your thighs?"

"It's my boyfriend's jersey number," she said. "He likes to call it out whenever he opens up my legs."

"Well, your boyfriend's a peckerwood," I said.

But she didn't find that amusing, even though it's in the script. We were supposed to bad mouth the boyfriend for a while, her and I. But she just looked away, her chin dimpled up, and her face got all blotchy. I could see that she was about to cry, so I backpedaled. "Maybe this isn't such a good idea," I said.

Ellie smiled, but her eyes remained hard. She stared into the distant gulf. "Yeah," she said. She slipped back through the door. "He's a peckerwood all right."

And then I was left standing on the curb in the blazing sun. I could smell the water on the hot breeze. I could smell the exhaust from the cars on 98, and I felt very alone in the world right then, more alone than I could remember feeling in years. It just came to me right out of the sky. Just like that woman up in Alabama who got smacked with that meteor. It just slapped me all of a sudden. And I realized that I had not spoken conversationally to anyone—I mean besides Mother and the Cock-Doctor—for going on a year.

Except maybe the widows.

THAT NIGHT I WAS in the kitchen with Mother getting the shrimp ready to boil. I'd bought these fat whites, fresh out of the Gulf with the heads still on. Mother groaned, pulling a skillet of corn bread out of the oven. She had her crystals with her and the book open on the counter beside the sink. It was after Daddy left us that she got into that weirdness, going to all the conventions and the group retreats. She met the fellow space cadets out there, and she'd drag them back to The Royal Palms. This last one had dressed in long white robes. He'd shaved his head and kept a little red dot on his forehead, like an alien. This was the guy who brought us the crystals. He said they represented the duality of the human soul. Good and evil. Life and death. He said you could live forever if you just focused on the quartz within your mind and flushed all the obsidian out of your body. Mother liked him the most. But then one day he too hitched a ride on a moonbeam, and just like Daddy we never saw him again. They'd come and go. What about me, I used to wonder. Where's my spaceship come to blast me off of this coast?

"So did you make any progress on unit 10?" she asked.

"I think we're going to need to call in professionals," I said.

"Rodger says that's a bad idea."

"Well the Cock-Doctor is a jackass," I said. But I knew as

well as he did what would happen if I called in the professionals. We'd get a whole squad of environmental engineers descending on The Royal Palms with fistfuls of exposure charts and regulation manuals. I could see the beakers full of ground water. The test tubes full of dirt. We'd need haz-mat certified contractors. Men dressed like astronauts. They'd shut us down at the height of the season, wandering the blacktop in their bunny suits and oxygen. "You know," I said—this was my angle—"the problem for me is mostly the headaches. The ammonia hurts my sinuses. You remember those pills Rodger left here last month? If you were to give me some of those pills, I think I could bear it."

"That's a controlled substance," said Mother. "It's dangerous and I'm giving those pills back to Rodger next time he's here."

"They're not dangerous," I said. "There's whole bureaucracies of the US government whose purview is to ensure their safety."

"Only under a doctor's care," she said. "What if you overdosed?" She tapped her chest. "I'd be on the hook for it."

"No you wouldn't," I said. "You could just tell the police that I found them. You could say it was the Cock-Doctor's fault."

"I wish you would stop calling your brother that."

"Rodger," I said. "You could blame it on Rodger."

"Fine," she said. "I'll give you one pill."

"I'm going to need more than one."

"Make good progress and maybe I'll give you more."

"Just tell me where you put the bottle."

"No," she said. "Absolutely not." She pointed to my boil. "Shrimp's ready."

WHEN I STEPPED OUTSIDE the next morning I could smell the water. I could hear the gulf rolling in the quiet air. To the east the sky looked pink with the sunrise. I walked through the sand and the grass to the side of the double-wide where I stopped to take a piss in the junipers. The world seemed calm and empty. When I came back to the pool, I saw Ellie sitting on the curb in front of unit 3. She had been crying, I think, and her face still looked splotchy, but she composed herself as I approached. From my pocket I took the pill Mother had given me. I held it up like a diamond in the morning light.

Her face burst with pleasure for an instant, then clouded over. "Just one?"

"I've got to clean out that unit," I said, pointing at number 10. "Then I'll get more."

"The meth lab?" she said. "I can smell it."

"That's right," I said. "The meth lab."

"Tell you what," she said. "You give me that pill and I'll help you." She was smiling now, wiping the tears from her cheeks. Standing, she held out her hand.

"Like a down payment," I said. I placed the pill in her hand. I thought she'd dry swallow it on the spot, but instead she shoved it into the pocket of her cut-offs.

"Let me get my stuff," I said.

A few minutes later I rolled up to unit 10 with a wheelbarrow full of cleaning supplies. I had Comet and dish soap. I had rags and scrubbies, a bucket of water, rubber gloves and a toilet brush. I had a ball-peen hammer and a pry-bar. Ellie was already waiting outside, dressed in a set of baggy mechanic's coveralls. I pulled away the caution tape. It ripped easily, and fluttered across the blacktop into the pool. I took out my thick ring of keys.

Inside, there was a smell like sugar and cat shit. But it wasn't just the chemical stench of the sludge buckets in the kitchenette. They had broken out the window in the bathroom and a possum had snuck inside and died. There were flies everywhere. Piles of Sudafed boxes heaped on the floor. I could smell the Dran-O soaked into the carpets. On the coffee table sat a two Coleman fuel canisters and a cardboard box full of gutted 12-volt batteries. There was a tank of ammonia next to the bed and another one set against the wall. I nudged the box of dead batteries with my toe.

"Nazi method," said Ellie. She pointed at the batteries. Our eyes were burning, and I could see Ellie wiping back tears.

"You're telling me Nazis did this?" I felt sick and dizzy.

"It's just the name," she said. She went into the bathroom.

"What do you know about it?"

There was daylight in the windows; shafts of dust stood in the mounds of garbage. My head was full of snot and slobber from the ammonia. But I followed her into the bathroom, watching as she opened the medicine cabinet, the drawers. She lifted the lid on the toilet tank. Next to the sink lay a blackened spoon and a lighter, a bag of cotton wads and a hypodermic. But there were no drugs to be found, and she started to sob again. These great heaves caught in her chest, and I could see her wince from the pain. I thought maybe to reach out and touch her, but I didn't. I justlistened to her cry. After a moment, she stopped. She seemed to buck up. "I don't know much about it," she said. "My brother makes it. He's—yeah. Look… let's just get to work, okay?"

"What's the matter?"

"Nothing," she said. "What's the matter with you?"

"All kind of shit's the matter with me," I said. "But I'm not the one cries all the time."

"So, you're one of those," she said. "I guess now you'll want to tell me all of your problems, right? Well go ahead. It's part of the service. But keep working."

So I did. I told her all about Mother and the Cock-Doctor while we cleaned. All through the day we piled up the garbage. The cardboard and the canisters. We threw it out to the Astroturf. We mustered the sludge buckets together in the kitchenette, and we rolled the tanks into the bathroom. Then we scrubbed the walls, the counters. We pulled up the carpet. We hurled the mattress out the front door. I told her my life's story. I told her about flunking out of college, and I told her about the women I'd known. How I used to fall into orbit around some girl, and wind up in Key West or Biloxi. Wherever it was her daddy owned a bar or a restaurant or a fishing boat. Anything I could weld or hammer, pour into a glass or fry up in a pan. I told her about my boy in Jacksonville. He's got be in the sixth grade about now, and how his mother used to let him call me around my birthday for a while. But he's given it up now. She's married again. And I guess this new fellow's a pretty good father, as far as fathers go. "I don't think he hits the kid," I said. "That's about all you can ever ask out of a father."

"And why do you live with your mother?"

"About every six months I wind up back here," I said. "I can install a toilet, and I can lay fresh carpet. The widows don't give me a hard time and I keep the units in good order. In the afternoons, I like to float in the pool with a cold can of beer."

"That doesn't sound so bad," she said.

We were in the bathroom. I looked out through the window, into the jungle beyond our property. "I guess not," I said.

"If you're so miserable about your life then change," she said. "Go get a job chopping cocks like your brother. He's got a wife, right?"

"Three of them," I said. "Builds 'em up out of scrap titties. And he don't chop cocks, he porks 'em out."

So we got to laughing about that for a while, and I guess we were having a pretty okay time together working on the unit and trying not to gag on the fumes. But eventually it got to be too much for us, and I noticed that Ellie hadn't spoken in a while. I went through the unit and found her in the kitchenette, where she'd gone quite green in the face. So, I pointed her to the exit, where we both staggered outside, our eyes and noses pouring out of our heads. Ellie fell to her knees. She vomited into the sand. I was squatting on the pavement, feeling no better. Dizzy and sick. I rolled to my back and I stared into the sky. The clouds looked watery through my burning eyes. I could barely breathe. After a moment, I rolled to my stomach too and threw up. Ellie lay in the sand next to me, a sprawl of gangly limbs. She stretched her legs, long and skinny, and I could feel them against my own. There was a wind, and she put her hands behind her head. I pushed myself to my elbow and looked down at her. The shadows of the butterfly palms played across her skin. She was a very pretty girl, beneath all the ink. Not that I'm opposed to tattoos, it's just that hers were brutal-looking, heavy and crude. She looked up at me in the silence, probing my face. "You don't like them, do you?" she said.

"I don't mind them."

"No, they're ugly," she said. "I know they are. My boyfriend's getting better. But he learned on me. I've got good ones too, though." And then she stood. She unzipped her mechanic's coveralls and pulled the zipper down past her breasts, where the coils of two ancient looking sea creatures spiraled around her nipples. Intricately scaled. Blue-green and shimmering. They were living things, thriving. Winding through the murk and silence. Even on her pale skin I could see them in the cold, lunar blackness of the great deep. She had begun to cry again, and big tears rolled down her freckled cheeks. For a moment I was speechless. Then I looked away, watching a flock of pelicans gliding east towards Eglin. There were gulls turning arcs over the water. I sat forward and stumbled to my feet.

"You hear about that bank job?" I said. "It was these boys who rented this room, you know? I saw them on TV."

She zipped up her coveralls. "Did you call the police?"

"Not yet," I said.

"Why not?"

"I don't want the hassle of it."

"I heard there was a man killed at the bank," she said. "Don't that matter to you?"

"Sure," I said. "But—"

"Well, it matters to me," she said. She began to sob again.

"What do you know about it?" I said. "Was it your boyfriend? Your brother?"

She steeled herself, closed her eyes. And when she opened them, she looked dead on at the door to unit 10. "Are they here?" I said, pointing down towards unit 3. "Are they hiding out in your room?"

"No," she said. "Come on. Let's get to work." She pushed back into the room.

"Wait," I said. But I said it under my breath, and she made no move to stop. She marched into the unit and began tossing carpet fragments out the door. I stood by the curb for a moment. But then I joined her, and we worked in silence after that, all through the afternoon. I was feeling highly conflicted about it. And I had a lot of fear too, but I can't pretend that I did not want to see those coiled beasts one more time.

THAT EVENING **I** FOUND Mother at the patio table watching Idol. She was tapping the quartz, rubbing the obsidian. There was some boy singing on the TV, and I suppose she must've been pulling for him through the crystals.

"I cleaned out the unit," I said. "You told me I could have more pills when I finished."

"You see they caught one of the criminals?"

"How about those pills," I said.

"What about them?"

"You promised me the bottle when I finished."

"The bottle?" Mother set her crystals aside. "What do you need the whole bottle for?"

"We had a deal," I said. "Clean the unit, get the bottle."

"We had no deal," she said. "I told you maybe."

"Mother, you said—"

"I said no such thing." She stood, gathered up the TV, and stalked into the trailer. I was left alone in the silence of her wake. I took her crystals from the patio table, fingered them a moment, then slipped them into my pocket. After a while I headed over to our sign, where I squatted to watch the road. It was quiet, and I could hear the gulf beyond the highway. The door to unit 10 was wide open, airing out. I would need a truck to haul off those buckets of sludge in the morning. It's hard not to wonder sometimes if that's all life ever amounts to. Maybe it's all just toxic goo to be moved from one side of town to the other.

I was thinking these things, with my hands shoved into my pockets, holding Mother's crystals and watching the sky mellow into the west. And it was only this faint rumble at first, some plane taking off from Eglin. They come in low over the trees, these fat, wide-bodied military jets, transports, and fighters. I've even seen the President himself, that massive 747 of his, flanked by four deafening F-16s. He'll come rolling over the pines, about a thousand feet off the deck. Maybe I'm out by the pool, clearing leaves or picking up litter. Just me and the widows. We'll look up, gap-faced and stupid, watching in unison as that tight wedge climbs over the gulf, like the winged chariot of some Bronze Age god. I glanced up, half expecting to see the President now, but it was just some routine C-130. Another of the lesser imps. Like me. And I let out this long breath of air, which I think perhaps I had been holding onto for all of my life. I shut my eyes and breathed.

"It is a night for us lesser imps," I said.

ELLIE SCOWLED WHEN **I** gave her the news. She was bitter. Her face twisted, and she began to tremble, to hyperventilate. Her sobs broke out in long, jagged wails. Then she bore down on her jaws. Her face screwed down tight. She was gripping a scream, an explosion. There was some final supernova of pure rage stuck in her chest. And she balled up her fist, and she punched me as hard as she could. I dodged a second blow. A third. I caught her wrists after that. I twisted her away from me.

"I'm sorry," I said.

"You pathetic piece of shit!" she said.

"I'm thinking this is a bad idea, anyway," I said. "I owe you something, though. Maybe I can come up with fifty dollars."

"A bad idea?" she said. "You're thinking this is a bad idea?"

"To be honest, I don't even know if I could," I said.

She stepped towards me, unzipping her coveralls. I was rooted to the spot, unable to move, and she grabbed my hands and pulled me to her breasts. I cupped my palms around them, sticky with sweat from the work we'd done. I could feel the hard knots of her nipples between my fingers. Her heart was crashing in her ribs. I could feel such a heat coming out of her. I don't know what I had expected, something cold as eels, a corpse girl, a ghoul. Something that had crawled up out of the ground. But it was heat that seemed to come pouring out of her, pouring right out between my fingers. All that heat. And I jumped back. I stumbled down the curb. "I don't need fifty dollars," she said. "I need pills. That old lady's got them."

I was staring at my out-turned palms as though they leapt with flame. "You know they caught one of those boys," I said. "I bet the Sheriff's putting the screws to him right now to find the other one."

"I reckon," she said.

"Where are we supposed to do it?" I said. "In here? Are we going to be alone?"

She didn't move, didn't jerk a muscle. Not the slightest flicker of her eyes. She just stared into me, with my palms out, like some dejected Lazarus by the side of the road. "We'll find a place to do it," she said. "But are you going to get me those pills or not?"

I CAME INTO MOTHER'S ROOM and sat on the edge of the bed. She had a copy of Dianetics cracked open on the blanket beside her and a pile of junk mail from various institutes and retreats. She had pamphlets on Tarot and channeling, another on the spaceship landing about to go down in Colorado. Some group wanted donations to build a saucer-friendly spacepad. She had her candles lit, her incense. She'd plopped the TV onto the corner of the dresser at the foot of the bed, and it was tuned to a show on witches. I patted her shin. She took her glasses off her nose, regarding me with that familiar contempt. But I wasn't taking it this time. I stood up and shuffled through the pile of clothes on the floor. I forced my way to the closet where she kept the mothballed steamer truck full of Daddy's old things. I pushed open the lid, and pulled from the trunk a couple of his Hawaiian shirts. His woodies and sand dunes. His big parrots and droopy tulips. I could still smell his tobacco and Aqua Velva. Sitting cross-legged, I pulled off my flip-flop and held it against the bottom of a shoe. In my mind he was a man who could take the moon in his fingers and blow it like a ball of dandelion. It amazed me to find that the size of our feet had now converged into one. He'd been my age, I think, when he left us.

"Why don't you throw all this shit out?" I said.

"Did you take my crystals?" said Mother.

"I asked you a question," I said. "Why don't you sell this godforsaken place and move down to Boca Raton with Rodger?"

"I would never do that to you. Now did you take my crystals?"

"I might've," I said. "Tell you what. I'll swap for the bottle."

"It's no good," she said. "I called Rodger and he told me not to let you near those pills and to flush them down the commode. You are now free of them, Cecil."

I shut my eyes. "God-damnit, Mother," I said.

"I'd like my crystals back now."

"It's no good," I said. "I called Pluto and they said not to let you near those crystals and to hurl them into the gulf. You are now free of them, Mother."

"You did no such thing," she said.

"I sure did," I told her.

When Ellie saw my face, she could tell I'd come up empty. I thought she'd yell at me again. And I got ready for her to smack me one. But in fact she just began to cry. She put her forehead to the concrete and banged it once. Then again, harder. And a third. "Stop that," I said.

She sank along the wall to the ground, where she sat cross-legged against the door, weeping and grinding her teeth. I could see her face flush with blood. And she began to hit the concrete with her fist. "I just don't know what to do," she said. I squatted and tried to take her hand, but she pulled free and pushed me away. When she spoke she sounded vague. Fading. "You ought to just go," she said. She stood and slipped back through the door. It clicked between us.

"Open up a minute," I called.

"If you knew what was good for you," she said, "you'd get a million miles away."

"It's that boyfriend of yours, isn't it?" I banged on the door. "If he's in there, I'm calling the police." I kept banging, but she didn't answer. "I can get through this door. I've got the damned key."

I took out my keys and I flipped through them. I looked at the door, then around at the pool, the other units. Nothing stirred. I could see the TVs glowing in the windows all along the motel. I put the key in the lock and that roused her. I heard footfalls on the linoleum. The weight of her body settled against the door. "You better not come in here," she said. I could feel the tumblers against the prongs on the key, but I didn't twist it. If he was in there. Hiding out. Armed. Well, then opening that door would be the culminating act in this grand pageant of idiocy called my life.

I pulled the key out and walked along the sidewalk to the road. I could ignore it all, I thought—it wasn't my problem. Or I could call the police, that's what the Cock-Doctor would do. I had reason to suspect that a murderer was holed up at the motel. It was my civic duty to call someone. But I felt unmoored. It was as if I'd stopped somehow, while all around me the great flood of suffering that is our life together had continued to roll across the surface of this sad little ball. Me and Ellie. My mother. Our roadside motel.

So, I marched back to Ellie's unit. I jabbed the key into the lock. I twisted and pushed through. I jumped back, expecting he'd fire off a couple of slugs into the night. Nothing. Then I peeked around the frame.

Ellie sat in the bed. She was on her knees with her face in her hands. I went inside and the door slammed shut behind me. I was about to speak, but then I jerked to a stop and dropped the keys. It was him in there all right. One of the damned meth-heads from unit 10. He was laid up in the bed. Ellie glared but said nothing, only cried. And I was gagging, holding my mouth in my hands. For it was truly an incredible amount of blood. A smell like wet iron. On the linoleum in the kitchenette. A godawful smear across the floor. And my heart kicked over. Pain jabbed in my chest. We've had guests die on us a couple of times. There was a frat kid once who drank himself to death. And this old man had suffered a heart attack out by the pool. Those deaths were both messy, vomit and shit. But this was on a whole new level. Blood had soaked into the carpet. It saturated the blankets and the mattress. But he looked peaceful, this boy. He lay with his arms by his sides. I felt my eye twitch and my vision tunnel. I knew I needed to sit down or squat or get outside into the air, and I put my hand to the back of the chair to steady myself.

"What the hell?" I said. The boy's eyes popped open. Ellie took his head into her lap. She began to stroke his temples, wiping at the sweat with a washcloth. I couldn't breathe. I kept gasping these ragged gulps of foul air. Slowly I sank to my knees.

He was shirtless, all but hairless with muscles. And covered in tattoos. A lion's head. An eagle in flight. An electric guitar. On his ribs, I saw the face of a girl. Spider webs and Celtic knots across his legs. I don't think he was watching me. I don't know how much consciousness he even had. Dreamy, soupy. I could see his lips move but no words came from them. He'd been shot in the stomach, a shotgun probably. The skin had sucked back upon itself, and these little red sphincters had bloomed around the ugly black pits. When he breathed, I could see blood bubbling in one of the holes.

Ellie could see that I was looking at his tattoos. "He's got a Viking ship on his back," she said, and they exchanged a long, silent stare between themselves.

"He's your boyfriend?"

She shook her head. "My brother," she said. "It was that fucker who shot him."

"The one they got at Sheriff's department," I said.

Ellie nodded. "I just need to give him something," she said.

"Mother flushed the pills," I said. "I'm not lying."

Ellie bit her lip. She held her brother's fingers. "You stupid son-of-a-bitch," she said, pounding him on the chest. "What the fuck were you thinking?" There were tears in the boy's eyes.

"He needs to get to a hospital," I said. "He'll die like this."

"He'll die anyway," she said. I looked at the boy's eyes as she said it, but I could read nothing in them, and what she said was probably true with his guts all shot up like that. "I just can't stand to see him in pain," she said. "He's my little baby brother."

Tears streamed down her face. She was shaking as she stroked his temples. He moved his head as if to look away.

"A man's dead, down at the bank."

"I know it," she said. "You think I don't know it? He probably had a sister too."

"And a mother," I said. "Maybe a little boy of his own."

"Will you just shut up? I know it already."

I stood above him, thinking to myself that he deserved this. I thought it was some kind of justice. But at the same time I could not help but feel a deep pity for him, and a sympathy, which I do not believe I have ever felt for anyone before. Such a damned waste of humanity too, this thing. His eyes darted between us but he made no sound. He just looked at us with these big, glassy marbles in his head. "C'mon," said Ellie. "Please, just help him."

"I don't have anything," I said. I reached into my pockets to turn them inside out. A gesture of proof. But when I opened my hands, I held Mother's crystals, one in each of my palms. Ellie took them. "What the hell are these?" she said.

"Mother's crystals."

"What are they for?"

"Good and evil," I said.

"This is the good one," she said, holding up the quartz. I looked at them in her fingers. They were very pretty to look at, with flecks of red in the scalloped surface of the obsidian. The quartz was shot through with milky thunderheads. Tiny rainbows glinted off the facets. I wished Rodger was there. He'd have taken over the situation. Done what had to be done. I merely felt sick.

"No," I said, pointing at the crystals. "It's not a matter of a good one and a bad one. It's just a matter of difference. That's what Mother doesn't understand."

"What do you do with them?" she said.

I scratched my head. I looked from the crystals to the boy, to the blood seeping from his holes. I didn't know at all what to do with them, but I took them in my fingers and I touched them to his wounds. I rubbed them in little circular motions, the way I'd seen Mother rub them. Then, after I had touched every one, I placed both crystals on the boy's forehead. He closed his eyes. I looked at Ellie and she nodded, and I took her hand in mine and I placed it over the boy's nose. Then I pinched her fingers together, and I set my hand over his mouth. We could feel him trying to breathe in quick, shallow jerks for bit. But it didn't last. And after a moment he lay still. That was all there was to it. Ellie took the crystals from off his forehead and she slipped them into her pocket.

We stood together watching the corpse on the bed for a while. Might've been twenty minutes we stood there. Ellie didn't cry after that. She was just breathing. I could see something bitter pinching at the corners of her mouth, but she'd gone numb, I think. Gone. Finally, she turned and walked out the door. I followed her to the curb, where she went first to her car. But then she thought better of that and just started walking. She stopped though, in the middle of the parking lot, and she turned to look at me one last time. I think she wanted to say something. I sat on the curb. I knew I'd have to call the police in a minute, but for a while longer I could rest in the silence of the night air. Then she turned and walked onto the highway. I listened to the bugs, the cars. Out over the dunes, I could hear the rolling waters of that unfathomable gulf.

THE ONYX SKULL

TIM DICKS

FINALLY WE HELD THE weakest among us to the deck while a shipman named Fernam drew a cooking knife across his neck. There was talk of choosing instead the captain, who was, by his authority, most responsible for our doom, but we were hungry, not murderous or vengeful, and so selected not the man most deserving of death but the man nearest it already.

Fernam used a cooking knife because we had by now abandoned our war blades in the hold or thrown them into the sea. Our victim, de Crasto, did not seem to mind, seemed if anything relieved that we remembered to open his neck before opening the rest of him. But in truth he likely felt nothing. For days his body had been slick with fever and in the final hours when hailed he could only roll his eyes.

We butchered him on deck and carried the parts below, to the cook's sandbox. We openly slavered in the flames' light but shared each piece as it was removed from the fire, likely for fear that anyone denied would begin considering the next supply. The thighs we cooked and ate first, then the meat of the calf, then meager strips from the man's breast and back and then, drunk with satiety, with men vomiting their dinner and taking it up again from between their knees, we placed the feet in the fire and ate even them. The head lolled near the sandbox and we left it there to watch the blaze as we shuffled off in search of dark places to sleep safe from ourselves.

I do not know who carried the head to the upper deck, but in the days to follow, as we returned to hunger but now without a man close to spoiling before us, we began to mind the head, balanced it atop a coil of rope near the stern and gathered close, as if it might ward against another feast. Had a wind carried in or waves struck our ship the last of de Crasto would have toppled and rolled but we floated in cursed calm, each day surrounded by the same fading blue in all directions.

And despite the passing of days and the sun's baking heat the head too refused to change, would not slack or darken or fester. We considered on quiet nights whether we might lift the perfect lids and find bright eyes beneath, peering and ready, sliding from one face to the next. Other nights, we debated the gain to be had by stripping the head, pulling muscle from jaw, even taking up the thing like a great apple and biting, tearing. But the flesh was by now poisoned or possibly sacred, the head granted special protection by God, left forever intact to remind us of our sin as we finished our starvation. When finally one of us rose to pitch the relic overboard we others were transfixed and insulted. We all had lain on the deck for days now, naked to the sun and stars, but as the man, Torero, approached the head, some of us sat and some even stood. Yet still Torero staggered to the thing and took it by the hair, looked to us for any objection, until the head's skin went slack and the skull slid free and knocked to the deck.

We came closer now and watched the skull roll to stillness at Torero's feet. The thing was dark, and not simply with gore but with a natural tint, a shine, as if polished and dyed to the deep black of stone. Wetness clung to it, and sinewy tissue. The eyes at least had withered and empty sockets stared up at us, welling with sunlight, and a noise stirred from the skull and its jaw fell open and it spoke.

The voice was low, a buzzing rasp, and neither it nor its language had belonged to de Crasto. After a few words it went quiet and remained so even into that night and even when we woke hours later to find the sky purple with lightning and the ship bucking beneath us. Rain carried in sideways and what garments I still wore had soaked through while I slept. Men had already risen all around and I stood and nearly slipped in water and then fell as a wave took up the ship's back, then her front. My head ached where it had connected with the deck and I slid back and saw other men scrambling and the skull tumbling toward me and I caught it.

Through the wind and rain and noise of waves we strained to make ourselves heard. Men yelled in joy and fear and finally someone went man to man asking for a compass, as if any of us might still carry one or even remember where the last had been left. We might have set the sails by the stars but all were hidden by storm. Some of us went to ropes anyway, and some of us lay back down to drift in the water at our feet. I watched as the captain himself climbed the bulwark and, without looking back at any of us, dove headlong into the clashing sea.

The skull I kept cradled close, and when the chaos became tiring I carried the thing below decks, into the tilting quiet darkness. Other men had wedged themselves into a tight space in the officers' quarters, which we had long since looted, and when still other men descended they carried lamps our way and were surprised to find us quiet and placid. Others stayed above to be whipped by rain and wind and to bay at lightning flashes and it was these who hours later sighted the dark low shadow of land. They called us to the deck but by now we were unable to grip ropes or even lower the boats before the beach loomed wide before us and rocks tore into the ship's belly and we all lost our feet and tumbled to the deck, some from high in the ropes.

WHEN THE SHIP WAS still we waited out the rest of the storm below, gathering what equipment might be worth carrying ashore. Men told other men where we had washed to land: Ethiopia or a mass of islands close to our original destination or even mother Portugal. But when the storm passed and we climbed back above the alien quality of the land was evident in the shapes of its trees, the quick rise of its beach into hills, and in the smell and the weight of its air.

Boats lowered, we descended the ladder and more than one man lost his grip and plunged silently into water studded with rocks. The skull I carried in a pouch made from a shirt and tied to my belt and it bobbed and knocked against my leg as I descended. Most of us were too weak to row and sat idly quaking as tide carried us into the sand and rocks. Then we waded over the beach, over stones and earth felt for the first time in months. I fell to press myself to sand while others carried on into the scrubby grass and still others, drawn by hunger, continued into the shadowy trees. While they thrashed the growth I rubbed my face into sand and wondered if I might worry loose the flesh, free my own skull inside, and would it too reveal an impossible hue?

After some time, when the shouts had faded, my soul unwound itself and began to drift free. First my body felt light, then heavy, then like nothing, and I was above, looking down at a skeleton surrounded by other skeletons on the shore of a distant land. The shirt I'd pulled on prior to landing was a sailcloth draped over my frame and the pants would have blown from my legs if not for the belt. I bobbled around overhead and may have drifted off entirely, was tempted to, but for the scratching call of the skull, just below, wound in cloth on the sand by my hip.

"Soro," it said. My name, but not even my name, a cutting of it, something a childhood friend had called me a decade before.

"Yes," I breathed into the beach, my voice weak, dry.

The skull was silent a moment. Then, again: "Soro."

Then also came the voices of men, running from the trees. Commotion, men dragged to feet, then me, pulled by hands to stand, dragged onward, protesting while my captor laughed, the skull now silent and banging against my thigh. We pressed onward through slapping and scratching branches and weedy razors and emerged finally into a clearing where men huddled close and spoke loudly enough to hurt the ears. A shipman had spotted and chased and killed with a rock an animal which none of us recognized but which each of us was eager to consume, and now the hunter was as jovial and lordly as a governor, squatting before the corpse with someone's dagger in the beast while others grinned and slapped his shoulders and still others stumbled into the clearing with more wretches from the beach.

The creature's pelt had been sawn away and the animal now was a pink thing like a large rat or a cat. The head man, the hunter, worried a cut from the body and handed it, trailing tissue, to one of the men closest to him. Then another cut for another, and another, and finally, just as the sun failed overhead, for me. I stuffed the meat into my mouth and its juiced filled even the gaps between my teeth and I felt ready to weep. Then this man who had seen and overtaken the prey and who squatted before us butchering it dealt out another round of meat and like a saint did not take any for himself until all attendant had fed again. The feeling in that little clearing was like one felt at mass or in a dream of primal times. We slept each of us better for it, and for the taste of meat and the wet of it in our mouths and the weight of it in our bellies.

THE NEXT MORNING **I** woke in a ditch, having rolled down a hill until caught by gravity and a puff of grass. I turned over and stretched under the sun, cold and sore but at ease for the first time in weeks, more comfortable even than during my first night aboard the ship.

The morning sea's stillness was a marvel. The sky was clear and the water beckoned with its shine, the color of a placid jewel cool in the hand. I might have waded into it had other men not stirred and stood and stamped around and finally moved uphill, toward the trees. Together we walked toward the noises of our own language unseen through leaves and even before we emerged again into yesterday's clearing, even while we stepped over fallen branches and patches of mud and watched for snakes in shadows, we knew by the excited voices that someone had again found food.

And it was him again, the same who had found last night's dinner. Only now he did not squat before a kill but sat against a tree, as did those around him, and amidst them all on a stripped log lay the animal's remains. When the hunter saw us he rose to his haunches and walked on knees to the meat and sawed us fresh cuts. Another man pointed a metal cup toward a stream he promised was close by. "Fresh, go drink," he said, and I had already taken steps before I realized he meant for us to take the cup. We found the stream and its water was not as clear as the rainwater we had captured in the early days of our voyage but was sweet and filling still and tasted sharply of dirt. One of the men knelt and dipped his face and so did another and then I too knelt, then felt the skull's weight rest against the earth. I fingered the pouch, thinking I would not dip my own head if I would not also dip our friend's, then eyed the other men, who eyed me, and thought better of it, and stood.

Back at the camp, the animal carcasses had been further divided into narrow strips. These the hunter indicated with his knife and each of us knelt and took one slick and vital and placed it in our mouths and chewed and sat so that a tight circle drawn of every man who had staggered ashore formed itself in the woods.

"There are more," said the hunter. By now the log was empty of flesh but he hunched close with his knife's tip in the wood and twisted so that splinters rose and curled. "An abundance of these creatures. Today we go in pairs to hunt." He drew back the blade and knocked a bearing into the air. "And learn more of this place. Return here at mid-day to feast. I will stay with two others to build a cook fire."

The hunter began assigning pairs but I had my partner and we slipped away, over the stream and then up a small rise, aware that now we were in unseen territory. Soon the voices of other men grew distant behind us and then quiet and I carried on through the thick terrain, uneasy, the skull shifting in its pouch against my leg. I kept eyes to the ground, ready for any signs of movement, and each time I looked up the land all around was mirrored, trees in every direction and the hint of the sun overhead lost in foliage. After enough time I began to wonder if I was moving at all or was sun-struck back on the ship's deck, if we had never made land and were in fact still floating at sea and dying in deepest delirium, would continue to float for years, until we crashed to a distant shore or the wood of our hull rotted and our corpses swam to the ocean floor.

But my body was sore, and not burned but cool in the shade of the trees, and the sun sparkled wetly through the ceiling of clasping leaves, and I was here in this land, now spans distant from other men but linked to them by a series of steps that would carry me back through the growth, over my own scooping steps in mud and thorns. And when I returned, hours later, I encountered two new proofs of reality: the laughing calls of the other men and the smell of fire and cooking meat, so irresistible that I clawed heedless through weeds, thorns tearing flesh, drawing blood into which mosquitoes settled before I had even stopped moving.

The fire was small but strong and men crowded close to its licking flame. As I approached some moved back and I saw the hunter tending a branch which skewered little bits of flesh. Small animals, some prepared and others still wearing their skins, lay close to hand on a pile of rocks. Talk quieted and most or all men looked my way and then the hunter laughed.

"Place yours in the row, friend," he said, and indicated my cargo. "We'll eat them all or burst."

I took up the pouch in one hand, holding it from the bottom so I could feel the spine's terminal bump. "This is de Crasto."

One man said, "De Crasto is at sea."

"At sea," I said, and slapped at my stomach. "The parts of him we did not eat are in the ship. Around the cook pit. Except for this." And I lifted the head, still in its pouch.

"Leave it," said the hunter.

"We heard him speak," I said. Their mouths drew tight, and I said, "I have heard him since."

"I knew a miner," one of the men close to the hunter said, after a time. "Cave in started and he goes stampeding with everyone to the surface. Only he's fast and gets in the front when it all comes down. Pinned his leg to the hip and crushed every man behind him. Only after enough time waiting for someone to come he starts hearing the other men back there calling up. Asking him to pass back some food. Not an hour and already this man was playing at hallucinations."

"Just last night," I said. But then the hunter raised his hand, the one not holding the knife.

"Toss it away," he said. "Not to the sea but into the grass. Or find a pit. Bury it."

"Here?" I felt at the pouch, thumbed the ridge of the eye hole. Inside, that shining ebony skull, that impossible sculpture. "In an unknown land."

"We're likely to all be buried here," said a man close to the hunter.

"Lucky to be buried at all," said another.

But now the hunter was on his feet, face red and knife ready. "You plan already to die here?" he asked one of the men, and for a moment he looked ready to strike, to bury his weapon in this doubter's chest. But then he turned to the rest of us. "You have no ability in your arms to hunt? In your legs to find the nearest village?" He went forward, looked ready to kill us all, then to a man opposite me and reached for him, took something from his hands, threw a fistful of meet into the trees. "You expect to die, yet you eat."

A cry went up then, and I thought the group might descend on him as they stood, but instead one man stepped forward and proclaimed his intent to live and prosper in this land, then another shouted his intention to strike out the next morning in search of civilization. Others rose and spoke of their indomitable hearts and of the certainty that with a week's work we would find friends and with a year's patience we would return to our homes. The hunter pointed his long knife at each man as if christening or knighting him, pausing to stare down the blade's edge and into our eyes. He did not aim the blade at de Crasto.

SOME MEN HE SENT to begin a new hunt and some he sent back to the ship, to paddle out and climb its ladders and pilfer its stores. When we returned that night it was to another feast of the small beasts infesting this land and there was no talk of earlier and we ate again until our fingers were slick with grease and then built up the cook fire until the flame danced and we passed around cups filled with watered wine. We, even I, bellowed songs and challenges to the shadowy trees and stalked the edges of our clearing, swinging weapons carried back from the ship. Some men now wore full swords and two carried crossbows with no bolts. I had found an officer's dirk, a weapon useless for hacking at thorns and grass but good for stabbing shadows, and kept the little blade tucked into the same belt that held the skull at my side. I drank more wine as men raged and howled and lowered themselves to the earth and finally lowered myself with them but later woke to find the fire low and all the men, even the hunter, asleep, and I rose and moved in the darkness and finally made for the low crash of the beach and there, in a place where the sandy earth was cool and malleable, made a new bed for myself. And from his pouch I took de Crasto.

I looked for a change in the skull's color or material but still the thing was of a polished darkness and cool in my hands. I pulled weeds to pile near my head and placed the skull in a low mound of them and stared into its eyes and it did not stare back and did not speak.

I stared at the skull so long that its angles and the wells of its eyes took on a cutting clarity. Then after more time the thing sank into darkness and was merely a shadow I could seize upon each time I felt the ground begin to cave beneath me. Finally I reached for and touched the skull's cool crown. With my other hand I reached behind my own head, dug in the hair and discovered a seam in the flesh, a sickening wet tear, and through this fissure took my own skull and traded it for de Crasto's.

Then I was back on the sea, on the ship, cutting fast and smooth through chopping but brilliant water.

Then I was over the beach and my sleeping self and over the canopied trees covering my drunken sleeping companions and over the sharp diving hills beyond.

Then I was slowing and land stretched in all directions and was surrounded on all sides by water. Far below was the entirety of the island, its beaches and trees and hills all as one. Then a heat warmed my eyes and a light burned from somewhere just out of sight and when I looked below the island took on the color of blood or flowers and one spot particularly, deep in the island and too far below to see with clarity, burned with roseate fury.

Then a jiggling of the shoulder, heavy breathing close by. I awoke to the smell of earth and grass and rolled to my back to see two men close by, squinting in morning sun.

"Lord Christ," said the one standing.

The other, squatted near me but looking at the skull, said, "What are you doing out here with this thing?"

They looked ready to strike or to kick the skull into the trees or the surf. I said, "A wake. Before burying him."

The squatting man stood. He was without a shirt and the curling dark hair on his shoulders caught the morning sun. He said, "We're all going out. Parties of four to press what we know of this place."

"The head man thinks we're in Australia," said the other.

"We are not," I said, but there was no way to explain how I knew the smallness of the island, that we were on a narrow rock slashing an empty sea. So I rose. The earth where I'd lain was flattened and the weeds there bent never to straighten. When the two men turned to move up the hill, back toward the trees, I stooped and took up the skull.

At the clearing we found two men tending a fire and the hunter himself standing with arms crossed as if awaiting our return. He would command me to bury the skull, I knew, but when we drew close he inclined his head, spoke to the man without the hairy shoulders, called him Lopo, which I was sure was not his name.

"The men have gone," he said, as if the present fire minders were not to be considered. As if he was not. He looked toward the silent tree line as if consulting notches sliced into bark or hanks tied to branches and then sliced the air with his hand. With that, the hairy man strode out and Lopo followed and I followed him.

For a long time we moved in jerky silence, stepping high over logs and sidling through thorns. After enough cuts and sweat the two began to complain of their wine sickness, of how poorly they'd slept, and finally Lopo reached for his side, where he had tied a skin which we stopped to share.

"Your name," I said. "It is not Lopo."

"Lopo," he said, as if this was an answer.

"And you?" I said to the hairy man.

"Baltasar." He lifted the skin and poured so it filled his mouth and ran down his neck. He grinned at the waste. "Or Martim."

Now Lopo took back the skin. For a time we passed it among ourselves. On the trees nearby and on every surface at our feet and leaping to alight on us tiny beings chased each other in patterns one might predict with enough observation. We all three were damp with sweat and it was easy to imagine these insects foundering in the wet of our bodies.

"I can scarcely see the sun for these trees," Lopo said. "We're to walk until mid-day and what if mid-day passes us?"

"We could stay here," said Baltasar. "Claim to have roamed and found nothing. Which is what we'll find if we keep on."

"That's what the hunter aims to disprove."

"Note that he did not join us."

"He's holding the camp."

Baltasar took the wine and drank. Displeasure showed on Lopo's face. Baltasar said, "We'll return with no news and what do you think will happen tomorrow?"

"Would you rather lie down to die on the beach?"

I realized my hand was sliding over the skull, over its pouch. Its surface was smooth but the bag was rough, worn, and I might have been running my hand over the sand of the beach again, might still have been asleep. Dreaming. The entire island spread out before me again and I could see how it was different in places, how the land rose and sank and choked into forest and gave for long tracts of open grasses and smashed in every direction against the thick green of the sea. "There's a long rise ahead," I said, and as I did I saw what was on its other side: a descent, and another rise, and in this rise's side something special, unknowable, irresistible. This vision laid itself over my sight like a scene caught dimly in a glass so that every detail revealed itself but smeared when considered directly.

"And?" said Lopo.

But I was in the dream, looking down at that pink stain over the landscape, and knew that whatever awaited us would not just save us but would also be what had brought us here, what had stilled the winds those weeks ago and led us to eat de Crasto. And only through de Crasto's eyes had I seen where it lay.

"Is this from the hunter?" Baltasar said.

"It is from the skull."

"From the skull," Baltasar said.

"The skull," Lopo said, and reached for it at my side, and stopped when my eyes caught his. For a moment we stood unmoving and if he had drawn closer I may have brandished the dirk. But Baltasar spoke:

"Now we follow the commands of a dead man."

We struck out again, first jovial, passing the skin, then quiet as the land rose and the trees grew sparse and our bodies began to burn in the sun. Each step spread ache through my legs but also brought the dream more fully to mind and I retraced it from my place in the sky back to the ship to the beach where I'd slept. If I really had risen above this land to see something miraculous far below then had I really replaced my own skull with de Crasto's? I reached into my hair to feel for a scar and found only bits of leaf and weed and resting insects.

We already dripped with sweat but now we festered. The ground swept ever to the sky and we pressed on until each step seemed a promise of imminent collapse. Finally Lopo stopped and I thought he would drop into the tall grass but he lifted the wine skin and squeezed a narrow dark trickle from it and then took another step.

"I could use water," he said.

"You know what I'd like more than water?" Baltasar said. "A woman. Right now if choice was given of new ship at beach or woman in the trees I'd wave you all godspeed."

"Maybe that's where the skull's leading us," Lopo said. "A field of virgins."

"In this sun they'll be darker than your teeth."

"This came to you in a dream?" Lopo said, now to me, as if we had not just discussed this. "I once dreamt I was a cat." But then: "And what is it we're meant to find?"

"Something we would not even be able to imagine."

"I hope you can spy it from the top of this hill because that is as far as I go." He raised the skin again and this time got nothing.

"You think there's any chance it might truly be women?" Lopo said, but neither Baltasar nor I answered and afterward we each worked in silence. As the trees continued to thin the grasses grew thicker and the ground more uneven so that sometimes earth gave beneath our weight and we would tumble to scrape our hands or faces in hardened mud and rocks. Lopo began to swear and Baltasar to hum and then sing in a way that betrayed a mounting anxiety and I with each step forgot my certainty only to remember it when the skull in its pouch slid against my thigh. The air seemed now not only hotter but thinner so that we were not only thirsting and hungry but also suffocating. Overhead the sky was a spread of pure blue and I realized first that no trees covered it anywhere I could see and second that we had nearly reached the peak.

All around land fell away and the island was spiked and long and narrow so that the sea sparkled on all sides, not still but rippling with waves that would carry us from here if only we had a worthy ship. We all made revolutions and I took in the distant hills and the valleys filled with trees of the most shadowed green and it seemed impossible that within some of them our fellows walked and within one of them far back, near where land met sea, the hunter and his closest huddled. And then there was the ship, startlingly clear against the frothing water of the beach, still tall and wide but undeniably listing, the great gashes in its side exposed to light.

"Look," Baltasar said.

"I am looking," I said.

But he took my arm and turned me and for a moment I was so struck with beauty that I didn't see as he did. Then the fall in the land ahead revealed itself to me, steep yet gentle, a slope to mirror the one we'd ascended, harsh rocks and earth softened with grasses. It was as in my memory but now clearer, in brilliant color. I reached for the skull and held it close and prepared to argue Lopo and Baltasar into further exploration but found them rapt, peering still, and by following their example I saw far below, in the shadows of the trees where they looked, among the many small hills and piles of fallen earth, a little hole in the world, a miniature cave, and before its gaping door, balanced on a little mound, a great smooth stone, somehow too perfect and perfectly placed to be natural.

"De Crasto wanted to tell us something," Baltasar said.

"He," Lopo said, but then he abandoned speech and sparked down the hill, leaping over rocks and kicking at tall grass. Joy and anticipation, emotions so alien that they felt like fire in my chest, built and filled me and just as I prepared to follow Lopo down the hill he yelped and fell into weeds, out of sight. Baltasar and I ran to him and I was sure at first that he had tripped over a rock and would spring back up and then, as we drew closer, that he had fallen through some hole into a hell just below our feet, but we found him twisting silently in the grass, clutching a knee to his breast. He massaged the bare meat of his calf, muddling dirt with a tongue of fresh blood licking along the skin.

Baltasar dropped and swatted Lopo's clutching hands from the wound. "Snake," he said, and while I turned to look for weaving grass he yelled assurances to Lopo, who yelled oaths to the sky. "Yes, these expeditions!" Baltasar said, and the grasses around were still. Already we had descended enough of the hill that the view of the sea was lost behind trees. "This is the end, the last one."

"The island is empty of people," I said.

"Our Lord, our Lord Christ," Lopo said.

"We'll get you back to the camp," Baltasar said.

"The poison," Lopo said.

"They will drain it. The hunter will drain it."

Lopo barked, then again. The hunter was hours behind. I drew the dirk and marveled at its easy weight in my hand, at its luster in the light. I bent to draw the poison but Lopo kicked at the grass, then at my wrist, and I dropped the blade.

"He will help," Baltasar said, but already Lopo was scrabbling, rising. He looked down the hill to the cave, then up, the way we'd come, toward the screaming blue sky.

"Back to camp," Baltasar said. "Then we return."

Lopo looked ready to stumble down the hill, to roll himself toward the cave, but Baltasar rose and took his arm. I collected the dirk and took the other arm and together we ascended back the way we'd come. As we climbed I became certain that behind us the cave's mouth had begun to emit a red light, first radiant then diffuse, a color as pervasive and subtle as smoke from a long-dead fire. Between us Lopo was heavy and laughing. As we approached the peak he grew heavier and his laughter slid into sobbing. We began down the other side, past the first few trees, and as we passed into shadow he moaned and slithered from our grasp and only when he had fallen did I realize how tired his weight had made me.

"I'm fine," Lopo said, but he thrashed, ran a hand over his chest, neck to belly.

Baltasar knelt. His face was wet with weeping. "We'll get help."

"I'm lost," Lopo said. He caught my eyes, then reached for my shirt and grasped far short. His hand, I noticed, was bloated, and so was the other. My gaze led his own and he cawed and slapped his belly. Now I looked at the leg and saw that the wound was weeping, the flesh around it puffing and dark.

Baltasar noticed as well and drew his weapon, a short sword, but the tool was ridiculous and I produced again my dirk and found myself wondering who had worn it before the crash, the calm, before the launch, who had worn this weapon at breakfast with his wife months before, who had walked around his kitchen with the thing strapped proud and tight to his waist while he feasted and kissed and sang goodbye to his children. But Lopo howled and writhed and there was no time for reverie. I knelt and across his leg drew a line of blood from one fang's hole to the other. Lopo sat up, his face pale and wet, and he grasped the leg and I grasped it and together we squeezed and a bolt of sickness arced into the grass.

Baltasar was far back now, pacing and rubbing what hair grew on his face. "The hands?" he said.

Lopo raised his clubbed hands, ground his teeth. Tears seeped from his eyes and mingled with the sweat of his face. "Cut them, take them off."

Baltasar came close, reached toward me, not for the skull but for the dirk. He looked gravely down at Lopo as if he would use the stunted weapon to saw away the hands but finally bent and pressed its tip into one of Lopo's thick wrists. Only blood came out, and in a slow pour. Baltasar tossed the knife to me as if both it and I had failed him.

"One of us should go to the men," he said, and he rose to stretch his legs. With no more words he loped down the hill, toward the thick trees and into the hours between us and the others.

Lopo gave no sign of understanding where Baltasar had gone or of noticing when I sat next to him. His eyes were closed and he chewed nonsense language. "This thing," he said. "Not right, foolish. Should work the kitchen. Carry barrels. Big arms."

I stood and roamed a spiral in the hill, looking again for snakes, but the exercise felt useless. No snakes would strike me.

"Wine, wine," Lopo demanded. His voice was ragged but

there was no wine to bring. After some time he said, "Bring me the," and I felt certain he would carry on his clamor for drink but he said, "De Crasto.'"

The pouch was as sun-baked as the rest of me but inside it the head remained cool, smooth. I took the thing and balanced it on Lopo's belly and he gripped it in ruined hands and sighed with relief. We had torn off the remains of his shirt and the skull was a shadow against Lopo's skin, a perfect blot. Lopo's mouth opened to expose teeth long ruined and he moaned and you might have wondered if the man was being somehow healed by the skull but before long the stink of his waste soured the air and his chest no longer rose.

I might have moved to close his eyes but why? Overhead the sky was nearly afire with brilliance. What clouds drifted were so thin and pale they may have been faults in my vision. And Lopo was gone. His body looked to have forfeited thirty pounds in death. Atop his belly the skull looked weightier, so heavy I might not be able to lift it.

I LAY FLAT ON A plane far above the world and watched stars burn through the darkness. Everything and everyone was an unthinkable distance below and yet I felt a calm, a peace. When I turned to look the skull glowed bright with light from an unseen moon. Slowly the thing swiveled toward me and the braincase flashed and the jaw opened and the skull would speak.

Then I returned to myself. I was not far above the world and the sun was not gone, was in fact bright just below the peak behind me, so that it shot the sky and sent long shadows over me and Lopo and the reaching weeds. Close by, people crashed and a familiar voice sounded and Baltasar, looking wrung and red, stumbled from trees and gasped laughter and collapsed. Behind him strode another man and then the hunter, even he crowing with relief. The three of them were wet with exhaustion and dry with dirt and red with the blood of long scratches and cuts.

The hunter and his acolyte came forward, saw Lopo, moved toward him, stopped. The hunter looked to me then closed the distance and took the skull from Lopo's belly. "You did not even close his eyes." He held the thing to me, as if might speak in accusation.

"Unnatural," said the acolyte.

"He clutched it as he died."

"This skull." The hunter rolled it in his hands. As always, the thing remained dark, smooth, as if carved of worried stone. "It is time to bury our friend de Crasto." He tossed the skull to the acolyte.

I said, "It has shown me something exceptional beyond this rise."

"The skull has shown you," the hunter said. He turned to his man. "Find a place for it. Among the trees, no matter."

The acolyte stepped forward, the skull held close to his body. Baltasar and Lopo, one exhausted and one dead, lay between us. I took to feet and met the hunter's man and was armed aside with such force that I dropped back to the ground.

When I rose again the acolyte was moving up the hill, in the direction of the skull, and the hunter had drawn close. He danced to the side, grabbed for my shoulder. He had my left arm but my right was free and I took the dirk from my belt and sank it into his breast. He fell against me, hands clutching my shoulders, our bodies tight. Against my grip his blood pumped wet and hot and unending. He looked into my eyes and gaped. His smell was of clean sweat and summer and fresh water and sun. Then the man most trusted to save us released his hold and tipped to the ground.

The acolyte now was far up the hill, legs pumping in fury against the incline. Had he dropped the skull I would have given up the pursuit and left him to return to camp for whatever help he could find but even as I drew near he kept the thing close to his chest. His gait was long and high but he had run and walked hours to get here while I slept and before long our pursuit grew clumsy and he nearly fell. Shortly after he staggered and stopped entirely and turned, drawing his short sword, one of the finer weapons salvaged from the ship. Before he had even readied the edge I lunged and with my shorter blade took his throat.

He fell, and as his last noises bubbled from his wound his body slid a short distance down the incline. The skull tumbled farther and caught in weeds and because of its dark color may have lain undiscovered for years or, if this place was as unpeopled as it seemed, centuries. I kicked grass and even took up the dead man's shortsword to hack at weeds and finally uncovered the prize, staring into the sky, then at me, its jaw hung open in an expectant grin.

Then I held the skull and the blade. An idea presented itself in my mind, fully formed, as if given by another: I would make my way down the hill to where the bodies lay. Baltasar, ruined by exhaustion, had not risen in the chaos and might not even know what had happened. I would approach him slowly, as a friend, speaking idly of the skull, and then I would sink the longsword into his chest and extend the dirk, let him curl his dying fingers around its hilt. The others would trace our path before long, would find this new graveyard and rouse each other into bloody frenzy, and Baltasar would not mind accepting their wrath.

But there was no need to kill him. I had the skull again. Together we carried on up the hill, back to the apex, and found the air there as clear as remembered, the sky as wide and brilliant, and all around the edges of our sight the crashing sea. Behind us the bodies and ahead, far below, hidden by shadow and distance, the cave, the hole in the rocks. I might have lost my nerve looking at it but the skull was almost warm in my hands, ready, darker when I looked, the curve of its clean top shining with sun. Inside the cave there would be no light and the walls would be stooping and slanted and crusted with insects and drops unseen would yawn underfoot and unknown terrors would chatter and lurk but the hidden skull would be whole and intelligent and wise. I had with me and would always have the skull.

T](#) **HEN INTO THE CAVE.** Light spilled into a little rocky space and illuminated dirt and no apparent living thing but when my body blocked the light a scrabbling went up and revealed itself to be a frenzy of the island's small creatures, surprisingly animate, quick with life, sinewy muscles gliding beneath fur, moving low and wary like cats roused from sleep. Many quieted when I quieted and others darted for the cave's mouth and still others chased back into gloom and these last I followed.

Here light was scarce and I trailed a hand over the wall to guide my way. From nearby came scrabbling and chatter which echoed and revealed the breadth of the chamber and its depth. No drawings marked the walls and no scorch marks the floor but still the presence of intelligence was evident here, a former habitation by someone wise and patient. Then, as I proceeded, light faded entirely and so too did the noise of the creatures and I found myself enveloped in a darkness entire. Panic played at the skin of my neck and of my ankles and as if to run from it I flung myself ahead, grasped at a narrow gap between rocks, squeezed through. The span narrowed and ground against my hips and then even my wasted chest and I might have lost myself spiritually and bodily to the trap had I not remembered the skull at my side. With a great contortion I reached down to feel its weight, its smoothness, and for a time I relaxed and was held up only by rock. When I moved again it was with deliberation and now I progressed in grating pain and emerged with a suck of air into a space that called back from afar my footfalls and even the drag of my skin over stone.

In this new expanse I wandered at ease and kicked no obstruction and felt none also and chased without satisfaction the ghost of my own voice. With pleasure I began to lope, then to run through pure blackness, and felt as though I were no longer in this cave, nor on this island at all, nor even in my own body, but on another plane outside of any familiar. Around me burned no lamps or stars but illumination presented itself gradually in the form of beams and arcs of crimson glowing against the void. Then all faded and again I was in darkness and now with not my words but my breath echoing all around. I sat, rose after a time to pass back through the hall which had admitted me or to discover the opening to a new chamber and found neither. When I finished searching an hour or more may have passed and my blood pulsed wildly through my neck and I was no longer certain that any world but this blackness existed.

Then I sat again on the stone. Then I reclined.

Then I, without planning or intention, unfastened the pouch from my waist and from it took the skull. This I held above in both hands without seeing its shape or shine. When I lowered it to myself it weighed at first like a great stone and then like nothing and after a time it became impossible to imagine that the skull was anywhere near or that I had carried it in at all or that such a relic had even held shape in this world.

Then, after a long thoughtlessness that did not dip into sleep but into something near it or beside it, I became aware again of the skull's presence, not by its weight or any heat or noise or other signal but instead by the will of whatever inhabited this place. Although all around remained invisible, I could sense the presence of watchers in the distance, of hollow eyes and open jaws, of dark bone encompassing great sentience. A spirit came on me then, or more accurately on the darkness suffusing the space around, and I felt the communion of many souls both superior and familiar.

I saw then a vision in the blackness: I was to rise and carry the skull a certain distance and to lower it to a certain place. I would then exit this cavern into a world of my choosing. I saw first the cramping long room of my distant home, and smelled the earthy boil of a vegetable at long cook, and would have marveled at the familiarity of the place had I not been distracted by the call of a woman nearly forgotten but of dear importance just years before. Then the vision changed and I was offered sight of a larger home, a house set in the comfortable coolness at city's edge, and before me the spare furniture of my childhood, the very walls I had slapped against as I toddled and shouted and collapsed in wordless tears. Then another vision, this one fresher in my mind, of the ship and the men and of myself but all whole, hale, and around us the proud hulls and sails of the ships carrying our brothers, rendering the vast sky overhead and the ocean beneath inconsequential. Then another, of a shop where I had once drunk chocolate with a girl I hoped to bed without knowing fully how I might complete the task. And another, this one alien, of a time not yet experienced, in which I headed a crew of my own men, stood furious and sure in night against an enemy uncomprehended but doomed to fall before us. And another, stranger still, of myself in a time almost beyond recognition, old and tired, at ease, enjoying a cup of wine beneath a tree designed seemingly solely to provide me with shade.

Into any of these scenes I might have stepped. But a deception was at play, an effort to cause me to inter something holy in exchange for a trifling prize. I might leave the skull and step into the light of home and after weeks or months or possibly minutes wonder what force had delivered me thus and what I had forfeited for the boon. With the skull I might discover wonders greater than this hole or the sun of home and without I would be forever plagued by doubt.

As I considered the path to follow a noise presented itself, first as a subtle clicking, then a buzz, then a drone. For a moment it might have been the cacophony of insects woken from long sleep but then the noise strengthened and did not splinter into the clatter of wings but into words, unintelligible but beyond mistaking. I reached for the pouch and found it empty, flattened, and imagined the skull gone before I remembered its place on my chest. As if noticing my movements the skull thickened its words until its voice was like strong music and its echo like the noise of weather in low hills. When I caressed its top the bone was warm, then hot. I took the thing in both hands and sat and then stood and without fully inhabiting my own body or the skull or anything possible to bound I moved over the cave's floor. The chamber's narrow entrance presented itself now freely and with grace gave to my passage. The uneven floor flattened and guided my steps. The winding passages I had followed not long before straightened until speckled and then stained and then washed with light.

And only now did the skull quiet. Behind us stretched the darkening cave, back and into abyss, a tomb scarcely escaped and designed likely to snare us both. Before and around us spread the island, striking at the sky and furred with life. The buried mystery picked out in my dream was but a fragment of the power here and I with the skull and the skull with my strength would cover the length of this place and conquer its confusion.

But we would require freedom of the land, and the peace of sleep, and the luxury of time in which to plan, and these things we could not have while other men stalked and grumbled and fingered their weapons. Together we climbed the hill, and with surprising ease, my tired muscles made fresh again by time in the cave, even my mind as new and vital as if remade in the darkness.

At the summit we spied in the grass underfoot the bloodied body of the acolyte and, farther below, the twisting remains of the others. I held the skull in one hand and with the other bent to take up the long sword, an ungainly weapon but one necessary for the work of the next few hours. Baltasar had begun to rise, to press himself from the earth first with one foot and then the other. If he had not seen the hunter's death he had by now seen its result, lying in the grass beside him, and now he saw me, striding close, weapon flashing with brilliance. He would be first, followed fast by the others, each subdued without anger or remorse. Soon we would sit on the beach, disturbed only by the play of wind over sand and skin. The ruined ship would dance with flames, burning to the water as proof of my devotion. Then, when all was quiet, I would rise and the skull would rise with me. Darkness would be thick in the trees and sunlight would torment at the tips of peaks and in narrow and hidden places terror would claw at my mind but I would have with me and would always have the skull. Together we will carry on.

CONTRIBUTORS

CURTIS DAWKINS is the author of the collection, *Prison Ink*, forthcoming in 2014. He reviews books from prison every Friday at BULLmensfiction.com

TIM DICKS lives in Minneapolis and blogs at timdicks.com. His work has appeared in Uncanny Valley, Wigleaf, and matchbook.

DARRIN DOYLE is the author of the novels *The Girl Who Ate Kalamazoo* and *Revenge of the Teacher's Pet: A Love Story*. He teaches at Central Michigan University.

COLIN FLEMING writes for *The Atlantic, Rolling Stone, The Boston Globe Magazine, Slate,* and *Sports Illustrated,* and publishes fiction with the *VQR, Denver Quarterly, Boulevard, Michigan Quarterly Review,* and *The Southwest Review,* in addition to contributing to NPR's Weekend Edition. His first two books, *Dark March: Stories for When the Rest of the World is Asleep* and *Between Cloud and Horizon: A Relationship Casebook in Stories,* came out in 2013, and *The Anglerfish Comedy Troupe: Stories from the Abyss* is due in 2015.

MICHAEL HEMMINGSON, screenwriter, novelist, poet, playwright, literary critic, and guitarist—died on January 9, 2014 in Tijuana. He was 47 years old.

CHARLEY HENLEY received an MFA from the University of Alabama and a PhD from Florida State. He lives with his wife and children in Cincinnati, where he teaches at the University of Cincinnati. His fiction has appeared in *Best New American Voices, Another Chicago Magazine, The Greensboro Review,* and *Copper*

Nickel. Amazon.com's imprint, Story Front, has recently published his short story, Satellite Mother.

BRADY JACKSON is a graphic designer living in New York City.

RICHARD LANGE's stories have appeared in *The Sun, The Iowa Review,* and *Best American Mystery Stories,* and as part of the *Atlantic Monthly*'s Fiction for Kindle series. He is the author of the collection *Dead Boys* and the novels *Angel Baby* and *This Wicked World*. His new collection, *Sweet Nothing*, will be released in 2014 by Mulholland/Little, Brown. He received the Rosenthal Family Foundation Award from the American Academy of Arts and Letters and was a 2009 Guggenheim Fellow. He lives in Los Angeles.

ANTHONY MALONE's fiction has been published in *Murky Depths, The Delinquent, Lowestoft Chronicle, The Quotable, Mad Swirl*, Litro Online and many others and his short stories are included in the anthologies *Villainy* (Halls Brothers Entertainment), *Dieselpunk* (Static Movement), *Cup Of Joe* (Wicked East Press) and others. He has read at numerous Live–Lit events and recorded for London Link Radio. He lives in London.

JAMES-ALEXANDER MATHERS is the Lead Designer at *PRODUCT Toronto* magazine. In between freelance illustration and design projects, he runs the limited edition clothing company Pidgin. He is currently based in downtown Toronto.

DEVIN MURPHY's recent stories appear in The Cimarron Review, Glimmer Train, The Missouri Review, The Michigan Quarterly Review, and Shenandoah among many others. He is an Assistant Professor of Creative Writing at Bradley University.

ANTHONY SCHECTMAN draws and paints in Grand Rapids, MI.

CPSIA information can be obtained
at www.ICGtesting.com
Printed in the USA
FFOW02n0823140214
3601FF